Some Things Weird and Wicked

BOOKS BY JOAN KAHN

Ladies and Gentlemen Said the Ringmaster
To Meet Miss Long
Open House
See Saw

BOOKS EDITED BY JOAN KAHN

The Edge of the Chair
Some Things Dark and Dangerous
Some Things Fierce and Fatal
Some Things Strange and Sinister
Hanging by a Thread
Trial and Terror
Open at Your Own Risk

Some Things Weird and Wicked

TWELVE STORIES TO CHILL
YOUR BONES

EDITED BY

Joan Kahn

PANTHEON BOOKS

*Library of Congress Cataloging in Publication Data
Main entry under title: Some things weird & wicked.* CONTENTS: *Clayton, J. B. The white circle.—Wilkins, M. E. The wind in the rose-
bush.—Collins, W. "Blow Up with the brig!" [etc.] 1. Horror tales.
[1. Horror stories. 2. Short stories] I. Kahn, Joan. PZ5.S694 823'0872
[Fic] 75-35855 ISBN 0-394-83244-2*

*Manufactured in the United States of America, First Edition
10 9 8 7 6 5 4 3 2 1*

TO DAVID AND LEXY

Contents

Contents

Playmates

My Dear Uncle Sherlock

It's a Good Life

The Transferred Ghost

Biographical Notes

Introduction

THE CHANCES ARE PRETTY GOOD that as you read the stories in this book—no matter where you are, in your own home, on an airplane, or lying on the grass under a tree—you're going to forget where you are and everyone around (if there is anyone around you), and absolutely the only things that are going to seem real are the people and places you are reading about—*even if those people are ghosts.*

The stories cover a hundred years or so, but the ones from the past and the ones from the present will seem equally immediate, whether you feel yourself bound hand and foot in the dark cabin of a sailing ship, waiting to die, thanks to Wilkie Collins' "Blow Up with the Brig!"; or feel your fingers going numb in the terrible, terrible cold (which Jack London had experienced firsthand) of "To Build a Fire"; or huddle screaming in terror with the boy in Vin Packer's "Only the Guilty Run."

Some of the stories in this book are intended to scare you, some of them are intended to make you smile even while you're scared, and some of them are intended to make you shudder.

Though happily and hopefully most readers won't have to face terror in the real world too often, everyone needs to be scared occasionally. It's part of the way we're made. Think of the delight a very small child takes in hiding behind a chair to shout "boo" at the first person who goes past, or the pleasure that the wearers of Halloween masks get as they go about being terrifying, or how, ever since there was the first campfire to sit around, the atmosphere has been improved with a really nice horror story.

We need magic to leave the real world every so often. And the skilled writer can create a spooky magic world for the reader, one the reader can step into and out of at will, by opening and closing a book. To be sure, the magic of a good story or a good novel may not leave you the moment you stop reading. It may have stirred your imagination so strongly that you will walk around in the middle of someone else's mind for some time to come. And often, later on, something that is actually happening to you will seem much more real because of the memories of what you once read.

These stories are intended to scare you while you're reading them, *and* to haunt you a bit after you've read them—but the shudders you'll shudder are safely anchored to paper in this collection of a good many things weird and wicked.

J.K.

Some Things Weird and Wicked

JOHN BELL CLAYTON

The White Circle

There were times when I had no desire to kill Anvil.

As soon as I saw Anvil squatting up in the tree like some hateful creature that belonged in trees I knew I had to take a beating and I knew the kind of beating it would be. But still I had to let it be that way because this went beyond any matter of courage or shame.

The tree was *mine*. I want no doubt about that. It was a seedling that grew out of the slaty bank beside the dry creek-mark across the road from the house, and the thirteen small apples it had borne that year were the thirteen most beautiful things on this beautiful earth.

The day I was twelve Father took me up to the barn to look at the colts—Saturn, Jupiter, Devil, and Moonkissed, the whiteface. Father took a cigar out of his vest pocket and put one foot on the bottom plank of the fence and leaned both elbows on the top of the fence and his face looked quiet and pleased and proud and I liked the way he looked because it was as if he had a little joke or surprise that would turn out nice for me.

"Tucker," Father said presently, "I am not unaware of the momentousness of this day. Now there are four of the finest colts in Augusta County; if there are four any finer anywhere in Virginia I don't know where you'd find them unless Arthur Hancock over in Albemarle would have them." Father took one elbow off the fence and looked at me. "Now do you suppose," he asked, in that fine, free, good humor, "that if I were to offer you a little token to commemorate this occasion you could make a choice?"

"Yes sir," I said.

"Which one?" Father asked. "Devil? He's wild."

"No sir," I said. "I would like to have the apple tree below the gate."

Father looked at me for at least a minute. You would have to understand his pride in his colts to understand the way he looked. But at twelve how could I express how *I* felt? My setting such store in having the tree as my own had something to do with the coloring of the apples as they hung among the green leaves; it had something also to do with their ripening, not in autumn when the world was full of apples, but in midsummer when you *wanted* them; but it had more to do with a way of life that had come down through the generations. I would have given one of the apples to Janie. I would have made of it a ceremony. While I would not have said the words, because at twelve you have no such words, I would have handed over the apple with something like this in mind: "Janie, I want to give you this apple. It came from my tree. The tree

4

stands on my father's land. Before my father had the land it belonged to his father, and before that it belonged to my great-grandfather. It's the English family land. It's almost sacred. My possession of this tree forges of me a link in this owning ancestry that must go back clear beyond Moses and all the old Bible folks."

Father looked at me for that slow, peculiar minute in our lives. "All right, sir," he said. "The tree is yours in fee simple to bargain, sell, and convey or to keep and nurture and eventually hand down to your heirs or assigns forever unto eternity. You have a touch of poetry in your soul and that fierce, proud love of the land in your heart; when you grow up I hope you don't drink too much."

I didn't know what he meant by that but the tree was mine and now there perched Anvil, callously munching one of my thirteen apples and stowing the rest inside his ragged shirt until it bulged out in ugly lumps. I knew the apples pressed cold against his hateful belly and to me the coldness was a sickening evil.

I picked a rock up out of the dust of the road and tore across the creek bed and said, "All right, Anvil—climb down!"

Anvil's milky eyes batted at me under the strangely fair eyebrows. There was not much expression on his face. "Yaannh!" he said. "You stuck-up little priss, you hit me with that rock. You just do!"

Anvil," I said again, "climb down. They're my apples."

Anvil quit munching for a minute and grinned at me. "You want an apple? I'll give you one. Yaannh!" He suddenly cocked back his right arm and cracked me on the temple with the half-eaten apple.

I let go with the rock and it hit a limb with a dull chub sound and Anvil said, "You're fixin' to git it—you're real-ly fixin' to git it."

"I'll shake you down," I said. "I'll shake you clear down."

"Clear down?" Anvil chortled. "Where do you think I'm at? Up on top of Walker Mountain? It wouldn't hurt none if I was to fall out of this runty bush on my head."

I grabbed one of his bare feet and pulled backwards, and down Anvil came amidst a flutter of broken twigs and leaves. We both hit the ground. I hopped up and Anvil arose with a faintly vexed expression.

He hooked a leg in back of my knees and shoved a paw against my chin. I went down in the slate. He got down and pinioned my arms with his knees. I tried to kick him in the back of the head but could only flail my feet helplessly in the air.

"You might as well quit kickin'," he said.

He took one of my apples from his shirt and began eating it, almost absent-mindedly.

"You dirty filthy stinkin' sow," I said.

He snorted. "I couldn't be a sow, but you take that back."

"I wish you were fryin' in the middle of hell right this minute."

"Take back the stinkin' part," Anvil said thoughtfully. "I don't stink."

He pressed his knees down harder, pinching and squeezing the flesh of my arms.

I sobbed, "I take back the stinkin' part."

"That's better," Anvil said.

He ran a finger back into his jaw to dislodge a fragment of apple from his teeth. For a moment he ex-

6

amined the fragment and then wiped it on my cheek.

"I'm goin' to tell Father," I said desperately.

" 'Father,' " Anvil said with falsetto mimicry. " 'Father.' Say 'Old Man.' You think your old man is some stuff on a stick, don't you? You think he don't walk on the ground, don't you? You think you and your whole stuck-up family don't walk on the ground. Say 'Old Man.' "

"Go to hell!"

"Shut up your blubberin'. Say 'Old Man.' "

"Old Man. I wish you were dead."

"Yaannh!" Anvil said. "Stop blubberin'. Now call me 'Uncle Anvil.' Say 'Uncle Sweetie Peetie Tweetie Beg-Your-Pardon Uncle Anvil.' Say it!"

"Uncle Sweetie . . . Uncle Peetie, Tweetie Son-of-a-bitch Anvil."

He caught my hair in his hands and wallowed my head against the ground until I said every bitter word of it. Three times.

Anvil tossed away a spent, maltreated core that had been my apple. He gave my head one final thump upon the ground and said "Yaannh!" again in a satisfied way.

He released me and got up. I lay there with my face muscles twitching in outrage.

Anvil looked down at me. "Stop blubberin'," he commanded.

"I'm not cryin'," I said.

I was lying there with a towering, homicidal detestation, planning to kill Anvil—and the thought of it had a sweetness like summer fruit.

There were times when I had no desire to kill Anvil. I remember the day his father showed up at the school. He was a dirty, half-crazy, itinerant knickknack peddler. He had a club and he told the principal he was going to beat the meanness out of Anvil or beat him to death. Anvil scudded under a desk and lay there trembling and whimpering until the principal finally drove the ragged old man away. I had no hatred for Anvil then.

But another day, just for the sheer filthy meanness of it, he crawled through a classroom window after school hours and befouled the floor. And the number of times he pushed over smaller boys, just to see them hit the packed hard earth of the schoolyard and to watch the fright on their faces as they ran away, was more than I could count.

And still another day he walked up to me as I leaned against the warmth of the schoolhack shed in the sunlight, feeling the nice warmth of the weather-beaten boards.

"They hate me," he said dismally. "They hate me because my old man's crazy."

As I looked at Anvil I felt that in the background I was seeing that demented, bitter father trudging his lonely, vicious way through the world.

"They don't hate you," I lied. "Anyway I don't hate you." That was true. At that moment I didn't hate him. "How about comin' home and stayin' all night with me?"

So after school Anvil went along with me—and threw rocks at me all the way home.

Now I had for him no soft feeling of any kind. I planned—practically—his extinction as he stood there before me commanding me to cease the blubbering out of my heart.

"Shut up now," Anvil said. "I never hurt you. Stop blubberin'."

"I'm not cryin'," I said.

"You're still mad though." He looked at me appraisingly.

"No, I'm not," I lied. "I'm not even mad. I was a little bit mad, but not now."

"Well, whattaya look so funny around the mouth and eyes for?"

"I don't know. Let's go up to the barn and play."

"Play whut?" Anvil looked at me truculently. He didn't know whether to be suspicious or flattered. "I'm gettin' too big to play. To play much, anyway," he added undecidedly. "I might play a little bit if it ain't some sissy game."

"We'll play anything," I said eagerly.

"All right," he said. "Race you to the barn. You start."

I started running toward the wire fence and at the third step he stuck his foot between my legs and I fell forward on my face.

"Yaannh!" he croaked. "That'll learn you."

"Learn me what?" I asked as I got up. "Learn me what?" It seemed important to know that. Maybe it would make some difference in what I planned to do to Anvil. It seemed very important to know what it was that Anvil wanted to, and never could, teach me and the world.

"It'll just learn you," he said doggedly. "Go ahead, I won't trip you any more."

So we climbed the wire fence and raced across the burned field the hogs ranged in.

We squeezed through the heavy sliding doors onto the barn floor, and the first thing that caught Anvil's eye was the irregular circle that Father had painted there. He wanted to know what it was and I said

"Nothing" because I wasn't yet quite ready, and Anvil forgot about it for the moment and wanted to play jumping from the barn floor out to the top of the fresh rick of golden straw.

I said, "No. Who wants to do that, anyway?"

"I do," said Anvil. "Jump, you puke. Go ahead and jump!"

I didn't want to jump. The barn had been built on a hill. In front the ground came up level with the barn floor, but in back the floor was even with the top of the straw rick, with four wide, terrible yawning feet between.

I said, "Nawh, there's nothin' to jumpin'."

"Oh, there ain't, hanh!" said Anvil. "Well, try it—"

He gave me a shove and I went out into terrifying space. He leaped after and upon me and we hit the pillowy side of the straw rick and tumbled to the ground in a smothering slide.

"That's no fun," I said, getting up and brushing the chaff from my face and hair.

Anvil himself had lost interest in it by now and was idly munching another of my apples.

"I know somethin'," I said. "I know a good game. Come on, I'll show you."

Anvil stung me on the leg with the apple as I raced through the door of the cutting room. When we reached the barn floor his eyes again fell on the peculiar white circle. "That's to play prisoner's base with," I said. "That's the base."

"That's a funny-lookin' base," he said suspiciously. "I never saw any base that looked like that."

I could feel my muscles tensing, but I wasn't particularly excited. I didn't trust myself to look up toward the roof where the big mechanical hayfork hung suspended from the long metal track that ran back over the steaming mows of alfalfa and red clover. The fork had vicious sharp prongs that had never descended to the floor except on one occasion Anvil knew nothing about.

I think Father had been drinking the day he bought the hayfork in Staunton. It was an unwieldly involved contraption of ropes, triggers, and pulleys which took four men to operate. A man came out to install the fork and for several days he climbed up and down ladders, bolting the track in place and arranging the various gadgets. Finally, when he said it was ready, Father had a load of hay pulled into the barn and called the men in from the fields to watch and assist in the demonstration.

I don't remember the details. I just remember that something went very badly wrong. The fork suddenly plunged down with a peculiar ripping noise and embedded itself in the back of one of the work horses. Father said very little. He simply painted the big white circle on the barn floor, had the fork hauled back up to the top, and fastened the trigger around the rung of a stationary ladder eight feet off the floor, where no one could inadvertently pull it.

Then he said quietly, "I don't ever want anyone ever to touch this trip rope or to have occasion to step inside this circle."

So that was why I didn't now look up toward the fork.

"I don't want to play no sissy prisoner's base," Anvil said. "Let's find a nest of young pigeons."

"All right," I lied. "I know where there's a nest. But one game of prisoner's base first."

JOHN BELL CLAYTON

"You don't know where there's any pigeon nest,"
Anvil said. "You wouldn't have the nerve to throw
them up against the barn if you did."

"Yes, I would too," I protested. "Now let's play
one game of prisoner's base. Get in the circle and shut
your eyes and start countin'."

"Oh, all right," Anvil agreed wearily. "Let's get it
over with and find the pigeons. Ten, ten, double ten,
forty-five—"

"Right in the middle of the circle," I told him. "And
count slow. How'm I goin' to hide if you count that
way?"

Anvil now counted more slowly. "Five, ten, fifteen—"

I gave Anvil one last vindictive look and sprang up
the stationary ladder and swung out on the trip rope
of the unpredictable hayfork with all my puny might.

The fork's whizzing descent was accompanied by
that peculiar ripping noise. Anvil must have jumped
instinctively. The fork missed him by several feet.

For a moment Anvil stood absolutely still. He
turned around and saw the fork, still shimmering from
its impact with the floor. His face became exactly the
pale green of the carbide we burned in our acetylene
lighting plant at the house. Then he looked at me, at
the expression on my face, and his Adam's apple
bobbed queerly up and down, and a little stream of
water trickled down his right trouser leg and over his
bare foot.

"You tried to kill me," he said thickly.

He did not come toward me. Instead, he sat down.
He shook his head sickly. After a few sullen, bewildered moments he reached into his shirt and began
hauling out my apples one by one.

12

"You can have your stinkin' old apples," he said. "You'd do that for a few dried-up little apples. Your old man owns everything in sight. I ain't got nothin'. Go ahead and keep your stinkin' old apples."

He got to his feet and slowly walked out of the door.

Since swinging off the trip rope I had neither moved nor spoken. For a moment more I stood motionless and voiceless and then I ran over and grabbed up the nine apples that were left and called, "Anvil! Anvil!" He continued across the field without even pausing.

I yelled, "Anvil! Wait, I'll give them to you."

Anvil climbed the fence without looking back and set off down the road toward the store. Every few steps he kicked his wet trouser leg.

Three sparrows flew out of the door in a dusty, chattering spiral. Then there was only the image of the hayfork shimmering and terrible in the great and growing and accusing silence and emptiness of the barn.

The Wind in the Rose-Bush

*"But of course you didn't see her. You've been think-
ing so much about her that you thought you did."*

Ford Village has no railroad station, being on the
other side of the river from Porter's Falls, and acces-
sible only by the ford which gives it its name, and a
ferry line.

The ferry-boat was waiting when Rebecca Flint got
off the train with her bag and lunch basket. When she
and her small trunk were safely embarked she sat stiff
and straight and calm in the ferry-boat as it shot
swiftly and smoothly across stream. There was a horse
attached to a light country wagon on board, and he
pawed the deck uneasily. His owner stood near, with a
wary eye upon him, although he was chewing, with as
dully reflective an expression as a cow. Beside Rebecca
sat a woman of about her own age, who kept looking

at her with furtive curiosity; her husband, short and
stout and saturnine, stood near her. Rebecca paid no
attention to either of them. She was tall and spare
and pale, the type of a spinster, yet with rudimentary
lines and expressions of matronhood. She all unconsciously held her shawl, rolled up in a canvas bag, on
her left hip, as if it had been a child. She wore a settled frown of dissent at life, but it was the frown of
a mother who regarded life as a forward child, rather
than as an overwhelming fate.

The other woman continued staring at her; she was
mildly stupid, except for an overdeveloped curiosity
which made her at times sharp beyond belief. Her eyes
glittered, red spots came on her flaccid cheeks; she kept
opening her mouth to speak, making little abortive mo-
tions. Finally she could endure it no longer; she nudged
Rebecca boldly.

"A pleasant day," said she.

Rebecca looked at her and nodded coldly.

"Yes, very," she assented.

"Have you come far?"

"I have come from Michigan."

"Oh!" said the woman, with awe. "It's a long way,"
she remarked, presently.

"Yes, it is," replied Rebecca, conclusively.

Still the other woman was not daunted; there was
something which she determined to know, possibly
roused thereto by a vague sense of incongruity in the
other's appearance. "It's a long ways to come and
leave a family," she remarked with painful slyness.

"I ain't got any family to leave," returned Rebecca,
shortly.

"Then you ain't—"

"No, I ain't."

"Oh!" said the woman.

Rebecca looked straight ahead at the race of the river.

It was a long ferry. Finally Rebecca herself waxed unexpectedly loquacious. She turned to the older woman and inquired if she knew John Dent's widow who lived in Ford Village. "Her husband died about three years ago," said she, by way of detail.

The woman started violently. She turned pale, then she flushed; she cast a strange glance at her husband, who was regarding both women with a sort of stolid keenness.

"Yes, I guess I do," faltered the woman, finally.

"Well, his first wife was my sister," said Rebecca with the air of one imparting important intelligence.

"Was she?" responded the other woman, feebly. She glanced at her husband with an expression of doubt and terror, and he shook his head forbiddingly.

"I'm going to see her and take my niece Agnes home with me," said Rebecca.

Then the woman gave such a violent start that she noticed it.

"What is the matter?" she asked.

"Nothin', I guess," replied the woman, with eyes on her husband, who was slowly shaking his head, like a Chinese toy.

"Is my niece sick?" asked Rebecca with quick suspicion.

"No, she ain't sick," replied the woman with alacrity, then she caught her breath with a gasp.

"When did you see her?"

"Let me see; I ain't seen her for some little time," replied the woman. Then she caught her breath again.

"She ought to have grown up real pretty, if she takes after my sister. She was a real pretty woman," Rebecca said, wistfully.

"Yes, I guess she did grow up pretty," replied the woman in a trembling voice.

"What kind of a woman is the second wife?"

The woman glanced at her husband's warning face. She continued to gaze at him while she replied in a choking voice to Rebecca:

"I—guess she's a nice woman," she replied. "I—don't know, I—guess so. I—don't see much of her."

"I felt kind of hurt that John married again so quick," said Rebecca; "but I suppose he wanted his house kept, and Agnes wanted care. I wasn't so situated that I could take her when her mother died. I had my own mother to care for, and I was school-teaching. Now mother has gone, and my uncle died six months ago and left me quite a little property, and I've given up my school and I've come for Agnes. I guess she'll be glad to go with me, though I suppose her stepmother is a good woman and has always done for her."

The man's warning shake at his wife was fairly portentous.

"I guess so," said she.

"John always wrote that she was a beautiful woman," said Rebecca.

Then the ferry-boat grated on the shore.

John Dent's widow had sent a horse and wagon to meet her sister-in-law. When the woman and her husband went down the road, on which Rebecca in the wagon with her trunk soon passed them, she said, reproachfully:

"Seems as if I'd ought to have told her, Thomas."

"Let her find it out herself," replied the man. "Don't you go to burnin' your fingers in other folks' puddin', Maria."

"Do you s'pose she'll see anything?" asked the woman with a spasmodic shudder and a terrified roll of her eyes.

"See!" returned her husband with stolid scorn. "Better be sure there's anything to see."

"Oh, Thomas, they say—"

"Lord, ain't you found out that what they say is mostly lies?"

"But if it should be true, and she's a nervous woman, she might be scared enough to lose her wits," said his wife, staring uneasily after Rebecca's erect figure in the wagon disappearing over the crest of the hilly road.

"Wits that's so easy upset ain't worth much," declared the man. "You keep out of it, Maria."

Rebecca in the meantime rode on in the wagon, beside a flaxen-headed boy, who looked, to her understanding, not very bright. She asked him a question, and he paid no attention. She repeated it, and he responded with a bewildered and incoherent grunt. Then she let him alone, after making sure that he knew how to drive straight.

They had traveled about half a mile, passed the village square, and gone a short distance beyond, when the boy drew up with a sudden Whoa! before a very prosperous-looking house. It had been one of the aboriginal cottages of the vicinity, small and white, with a roof extending on one side over a piazza, and a tiny "L" jutting out in the rear, on the right hand. Now the cottage was transformed by dormer windows, a bay window on the piazzaless side, a carved railing down the front steps, and a modern hardwood door.

"Is this John Dent's house?" asked Rebecca.

The boy was as sparing of speech as a philosopher. His only response was in flinging the reins over the horse's back, stretching out one foot to the shaft, and leaping out of the wagon, then going around to the rear for the trunk. Rebecca got out and went toward the house. Its white paint had a new gloss; its blinds were an immaculate apple green; the lawn was trimmed as smooth as velvet, and it was dotted with scrupulous groups of hydrangeas and cannas.

"I always understood that John Dent was well-to-do," Rebecca reflected, comfortably. "I guess Agnes will have considerable. I've got enough, but it will come in handy for her schooling. She can have advantages."

The boy dragged the trunk up the fine gravel walk, but before he reached the steps leading up to the piazza, for the house stood on a terrace, the front door opened and a fair, frizzled head of a very large and handsome woman appeared. She held up her black silk skirt, disclosing voluminous ruffles of starched embroidery, and waited for Rebecca. She smiled placidly, her pink, double-chinned face widened and dimpled, but her blue eyes were wary and calculating. She extended her hand as Rebecca climbed the steps.

"This is Miss Flint, I suppose," said she.

"Yes, ma'am," replied Rebecca, noticing with bewilderment a curious expression compounded of fear and defiance on the other's face.

"Your letter only arrived this morning," said Mrs. Dent, in a steady voice. Her great face was a uniform pink, and her china-blue eyes were at once aggressive and veiled with secrecy.

"Yes, I hardly thought you'd get my letter," replied

Rebecca. "I felt as if I could not wait to hear from you before I came. I supposed you would be so situated that you could have me a little while without putting you out too much, from what John used to write me about his circumstances, and when I had that money so unexpected I felt as if I must come for Agnes. I suppose you will be willing to give her up. You know she's my own blood, and of course she's no relation to you, though you must have got attached to her. I know from her picture what a sweet girl she must be, and John always said she looked like her own mother, and Grace was a beautiful woman, if she was my sister."

Rebecca stopped and stared at the other woman in amazement and alarm. The great handsome blonde creature stood speechless, livid, gasping, with her hand to her heart, her lips parted in a horrible caricature of a smile.

"Are you sick!" cried Rebecca, drawing near. "Don't you want me to get you some water!"

Then Mrs. Dent recovered herself with a great effort. "It is nothing," she said. "I am subject to—spells. I am over it now. Won't you come in, Miss Flint?"

As she spoke, the beautiful deep-rose color suffused her face, her blue eyes met her visitor's with the opaqueness of turquoise—with a revelation of blue, but a concealment of all behind.

Rebecca followed her hostess in, and the boy, who had waited quiescently, climbed the steps with the trunk. But before they entered the door a strange thing happened. On the upper terrace, close to the piazza post, grew a great rose-bush, and on it, late in the season though it was, one small red, perfect rose.

Rebecca looked at it, and the other woman extended

her hand with a quick gesture. "Don't you pick that rose!" she brusquely cried.

Rebecca drew herself up with stiff dignity.

"I ain't in the habit of picking other folks' roses without leave," said she.

As Rebecca spoke she started violently and lost sight of her resentment, for something singular happened. Suddenly the rose-bush was agitated violently as if by a gust of wind, yet it was a remarkably still day. Not a leaf of the hydrangea standing on the terrace close to the rose trembled.

"What on earth—" began Rebecca; then she stopped with a gasp at the sight of the other woman's face. Although a face, it gave somehow the impression of a desperately clutched hand of secrecy.

"Come in!" said she in a harsh voice, which seemed to come forth from her chest with no intervention of the organs of speech. "Come into the house. I'm getting cold out here."

"What makes that rose-bush blow so when there isn't any wind?" asked Rebecca, trembling with vague horror, yet resolute.

"I don't see as it is blowing," returned the woman, calmly. And as she spoke, indeed, the bush was quiet.

"It was blowing," declared Rebecca.

"It isn't now," said Mrs. Dent. "I can't try to account for everything that blows out-of-doors. I have too much to do."

She spoke scornfully and confidently, with defiant, unflinching eyes, first on the bush, then on Rebecca, and led the way into the house.

"It looked queer," persisted Rebecca, but she followed, and also the boy with the trunk.

Rebecca entered an interior, prosperous, even elegant, according to her simple ideas. There were Brussels carpets, lace curtains, and plenty of brilliant upholstery and polished wood.

"You're real nicely situated," remarked Rebecca after she had become a little accustomed to her new surroundings and the two women were seated at the tea-table.

Mrs. Dent stared with a hard complacency from behind her silver-plated service. "Yes, I be," said she.

"You got all the things new?" said Rebecca, hesitatingly, with a jealous memory of her dead sister's bridal furnishings.

"Yes," said Mrs. Dent. "I was never one to want dead folks' things, and I had money enough of my own, so I wasn't beholden to John. I had the old duds put up at auction. They didn't bring much."

"I suppose you saved some for Agnes. She'll want some of her poor mother's things when she is grown up," said Rebecca with some indignation.

The defiant stare of Mrs. Dent's blue eyes waxed more intense. "There's a few things up garret," said she.

"She'll be likely to value them," remarked Rebecca. As she spoke she glanced at the window. "Isn't it 'most time for her to be coming home?" she asked.

"'Most time," answered Mrs. Dent, carelessly; "but when she gets over to Addie Slocum's she never knows when to come home."

"Is Addie Slocum her intimate friend?"

"Intimate as any."

"Maybe we can have her come out to see Agnes when she's living with me," said Rebecca, wistfully. "I suppose she'll be likely to be homesick at first."

"Most likely," answered Mrs. Dent.

"Does she call you mother?" Rebecca asked.

"No, she calls me Aunt Emeline," replied the other woman, shortly. "When did you say you were going home?"

"In about a week, I thought, if she can be ready to go so soon," answered Rebecca with a surprised look.

She reflected that she would not remain a day longer than she could help after such an inhospitable look and question.

"Oh, as far as that goes," said Mrs. Dent, "it wouldn't make any difference about her being ready. You could go home whenever you felt that you must, and she could come afterward."

"Alone?"

"Why not? She's a big girl now, and you don't have to change cars."

"My niece will go home when I do, and not travel alone; and if I can't wait here for her, in the house that used to be her mother's and my sister's home, I'll go and board somewhere," returned Rebecca with warmth.

"Oh, you can stay here as long as you want to. You're welcome," said Mrs. Dent.

Then Rebecca started. "There she is!" she declared in a trembling, exultant voice. Nobody knew how she longed to see the girl.

"She isn't as late as I thought she'd be," said Mrs. Dent, and again that curious, subtle change passed over her face, and again it settled into that stony impassiveness.

Rebecca stared at the door, waiting for it to open. "Where is she?" she asked, presently.

"I guess she's stopped to take off her hat in the entry," suggested Mrs. Dent.

Rebecca waited. "Why don't she come? It can't take her all this time to take off her hat."

For answer Mrs. Dent rose with a stiff jerk and threw open the door.

"Agnes!" she called. "Agnes!" Then she turned and eyed Rebecca. "She ain't there."

"I saw her pass the window," said Rebecca in bewilderment.

"You must have been mistaken."

"I know I did," persisted Rebecca.

"You couldn't have."

"I did. I saw first a shadow go over the ceiling, then I saw her in the glass there"—she pointed to a mirror over the sideboard opposite—"and then the shadow passed the window."

"How did she look in the glass?"

"Little and light-haired, with the light hair kind of tossing over her forehead."

"You couldn't have seen her."

"Was that like Agnes?"

"Like enough; but of course you didn't see her. You've been thinking so much about her that you thought you did."

"You thought *you* did."

"I thought I saw a shadow pass the window, but I must have been mistaken. She didn't come in, or we would have seen her before now. I knew it was too early for her to get home from Addie Slocum's, anyhow."

When Rebecca went to bed Agnes had not returned. Rebecca had resolved that she would not retire until the girl came, but she was very tired, and she reasoned with herself that she was foolish. Besides, Mrs. Dent suggested that Agnes might go to the church social with Addie Slocum. When Rebecca suggested that she be sent for and told that her aunt had come, Mrs. Dent laughed meaningly.

"I guess you'll find out that a young girl ain't so ready to leave a sociable, where there's boys, to see her aunt," said she.

"She's too young," said Rebecca, incredulously and indignantly.

"She sixteen," replied Mrs. Dent; "and she's always been great for the boys."

"She's going to school four years after I get her before she thinks of boys," declared Rebecca.

"We'll see," laughed the other woman.

After Rebecca went to bed, she lay awake a long time listening for the sound of girlish laughter and a boy's voice under her window; then she fell asleep.

The next morning she was down early. Mrs. Dent, who kept no servants, was busily preparing breakfast.

"Don't Agnes help you about breakfast?" asked Rebecca.

"No, I let her lay," replied Mrs. Dent, shortly.

"What time did she get home last night?"

"She didn't get home."

"What?"

"She didn't get home. She stayed with Addie. She often does."

"Without sending you word?"

"Oh, she knew I wouldn't worry."

"When will she be home?"

"Oh, I guess she'll be along pretty soon."

Rebecca was uneasy, but she tried to conceal it, for she knew of no good reason for uneasiness. What was there to occasion alarm in the fact of one young girl staying overnight with another? She could not eat much breakfast. Afterward she went out on the little piazza, although her hostess strove furtively to stop her.

"Why don't you go out back of the house? It's real pretty—a view over the river," she said.

"I guess I'll go out here," replied Rebecca. She had a purpose—to watch for the absent girl.

Presently Rebecca came hustling into the house through the sitting room, into the kitchen where Mrs. Dent was cooking.

"That rose-bush!" she gasped.

Mrs. Dent turned and faced her.

"What of it?"

"It's a-blowing."

"What of it?"

"There isn't a mite of wind this morning."

Mrs. Dent turned with an inimitable toss of her fair head. "If you think I can spend my time puzzling over such nonesense as—," she began, but Rebecca interrupted her with a cry and a rush to the door.

"There she is now!" she cried.

She flung the door wide open, and curiously enough a breeze came in and her own gray hair tossed, and a paper blew off the table to the floor with a loud rustle, but there was nobody in sight.

"There's nobody here," Rebecca said.

She looked blankly at the other woman, who brought her rolling-pin down on a slab of pie crust with a thud.

"I didn't hear anybody," she said, calmly.

"*I saw somebody pass that window!*"

"You were mistaken again."

"I *know* I saw somebody."

"You couldn't have. Please shut that door."

Rebecca shut the door. She sat down beside the window and looked out on the autumnal yard, with its little curve of footpath to the kitchen door.

"What smells so strong of roses in this room?" she said, presently. She sniffed hard.

"I don't smell anything but these nutmegs."

"It is not nutmeg."

"I don't smell anything else."

"Where do you suppose Agnes is?"

"Oh, perhaps she has gone over the ferry to Porter's Falls with Addie. She often does. Addie's got an aunt over there, and Addie's got a cousin, a real pretty boy."

"You suppose she's gone over there?"

"Mebbe. I shouldn't wonder."

"When should she be home?"

"Oh, not before afternoon."

Rebecca waited with all the patience she could muster. She kept reassuring herself, telling herself that it was all natural, that the other woman could not help it, but she made up her mind that if Agnes did not return that afternoon she should be sent for.

When it was four o'clock she started up with resolution. She had been furtively watching the onyx clock on the sitting-room mantel; she had timed herself. She had said that if Agnes was not home by that time she should demand that she be sent for. She rose and stood before Mrs. Dent, who looked up coolly from her embroidery.

"I've waited just as long as I'm going to," she said. "I've come 'way from Michigan to see my own sister's daughter and take her home with me. I've been here

ever since yesterday—twenty-four hours—and I
haven't seen her. Now I'm going to. I want her sent
for."

Mrs. Dent folded her embroidery and rose.

"Well, I don't blame you," she said. "It is high
time she came home. I'll go right over and get her
myself."

Rebecca heaved a sigh of relief. She hardly knew
what she had suspected or feared, but she knew that
her position had been one of antagonism if not accusa-
tion, and she was sensible of relief.

"I wish you would," she said, gratefully, and went
back to her chair, while Mrs. Dent got her shawl and
her little white head-tie. "I wouldn't trouble you, but
I do feel as if I couldn't wait any longer to see her,"
she remarked, apologetically.

"Oh, it ain't any trouble at all," said Mrs. Dent as
she went out. "I don't blame you; you have waited
long enough."

Rebecca sat at the window watching breathlessly
until Mrs. Dent came stepping through the yard alone.
She ran to the door and saw, hardly noticing it this
time, that the rose-bush was again violently agitated,
yet with no wind evident elsewhere.

"Where is she?" she cried.

Mrs. Dent laughed with stiff lips as she came up the
steps over the terrace. "Girls will be girls," said she.
"She's gone with Addie to Lincoln. Addie's got an
uncle who's conductor on the train, and lives there,
and he got 'em passes, and they're goin' to stay to
Addie's Aunt Margaret's a few days. Mrs. Slocum
said Agnes didn't have time to come over and ask me
before the train went, but she took it on herself to say
it would be all right, and—"

"Why hadn't she been over to tell you?" Rebecca was angry, though not suspicious. She even saw no reason for her anger.

"Oh, she was putting up grapes. She was coming over just as soon as she got the black off her hands. She heard I had company, and her hands were a sight. She was holding them over sulphur matches."

"You say she's going to stay a few days?" repeated Rebecca, dazedly.

"Yes; till Thursday, Mrs. Slocum said."

"How far is Lincoln from here?"

"About fifty miles. It'll be a real treat to her. Mrs. Slocum's sister is a real nice woman."

"It is goin' to make it pretty late about my goin' home."

"If you don't feel as if you could wait, I'll get her ready and send her on just as soon as I can," Mrs. Dent said, sweetly.

"I'm going to wait," said Rebecca, grimly.

The two women sat down again, and Mrs. Dent took up her embroidery.

"Is there any sewing I can do for her?" Rebecca asked, finally, in a desperate way. "If I can get her sewing along some—"

Mrs. Dent arose with alacrity and fetched a mass of white from the closet. "Here," she said, "if you want to sew the lace on this nightgown. I was going to put her to it, but she'll be glad enough to get rid of it. She ought to have this and one more before she goes. I don't like to send her away without some good underclothing."

Rebecca snatched at the little white garment and sewed feverishly.

That night she wakened from a deep sleep a little

after midnight and lay a minute trying to collect her
faculties and explain to herself what she was listening
to. At last she discovered that it was the then popular
strains of "The Maiden's Prayer" floating up through
the floor from the piano in the sitting room below.
She jumped up, threw a shawl over her nightgown, and
hurried downstairs trembling. There was nobody in the
sitting room; the piano was silent. She ran to Mrs.
Dent's bedroom and called hysterically:

"Emeline! Emeline!"

"What is it?" asked Mrs. Dent's voice from the
bed. The voice was stern, but had a note of consciousness in it.

"Who—who was that playing 'The Maiden's
Prayer' in the sitting room, on the piano?"

"I didn't hear anybody."

"There was some one."

"I didn't hear anything."

"I tell you there was some one. But—*there ain't
anybody there.*"

"I didn't hear anything."

"I did—somebody playing 'The Maiden's Prayer'
on the piano. Has Agnes got home? I *want to know.*"

"Of course Agnes hasn't got home," answered Mrs.
Dent with rising inflection. "Be you gone crazy over
that girl? The last boat from Porter's Falls was in
before we went to bed. Of course she ain't come."

"I heard—"

"You were dreaming."

"I wasn't; I was broad awake."

Rebecca went back to her chamber and kept her
lamp burning all night.

The next morning her eyes upon Mrs. Dent were

wary and blazing with suppressed excitement. She kept opening her mouth as if to speak, then frowning, and setting her lips hard. After breakfast she went upstairs, and came down presently with her coat and bonnet.

"Now, Emeline," she said, "I want to know where the Slocums live."

Mrs. Dent gave a strange, long, half-lidded glance at her. She was finishing her coffee.

"Why?" she asked.

"I'm going over there and find out if they have heard anything from her daughter and Agnes since they went away. I don't like what I heard last night."

"You must have been dreaming."

"It don't make any odds whether I was or not. Does she play 'The Maiden's Prayer' on the piano? I want to know."

"What if she does? She plays it a little, I believe. I don't know. She don't half play it, anyhow; she ain't got an ear."

"That wasn't half played last night. I don't like such things happening. I ain't superstitious, but I don't like it. I'm going. Where do the Slocums live?"

"You go down the road over the bridge past the old grist mill, then you turn to the left; it's the only house for half a mile. You can't miss it. It has a barn with a ship in full sail on the cupola."

"Well, I'm going. I don't feel easy."

About two hours later Rebecca returned. There were red spots on her cheeks. She looked wild. "I've been there," she said, "and there isn't a soul at home. Something *has* happened."

"What has happened?"

"I don't know. Something. I had a warning last night. There wasn't a soul there. They've been sent for to Lincoln."

"Did you see anybody to ask?" asked Mrs. Dent with thinly concealed anxiety.

"I asked the woman that lives on the turn of the road. She's stone deaf. I suppose you know. She listened while I screamed at her to know where the Slocums were, and then she said, 'Mrs. Smith don't live here.' I didn't see anybody on the road, and that's the only house. What do you suppose it means?"

"I don't suppose it means much of anything," replied Mrs. Dent, coolly. "Mr. Slocum is conductor on the railroad, and he'd be away, anyway, and Mrs. Slocum often goes early when he does, to spend the day with her sister in Porter's Falls. She'd be more likely to go away than Addie."

"And you don't think anything has happened?" Rebecca asked with diminishing distrust before the reasonableness of it.

"Land, no!"

Rebecca went upstairs to lay aside her coat and bonnet. But she came hurrying back with them still on.

"Who's been in my room?" she gasped. Her face was pale as ashes.

Mrs. Dent also paled as she regarded her.

"What do you mean?" she asked, slowly.

"I found when I went upstairs that—little night-gown of—Agnes's on—the bed, laid out. It was—*laid out*. The sleeves were folded across the bosom, and there was that little red rose between them. Emeline, what is it? Emeline, what's the matter? Oh!"

Mrs. Dent was struggling for breath in great, choking gasps. She clung to the back of a chair. Rebecca, trembling herself so she could scarcely keep on her feet, got her some water.

As soon as she recovered herself Mrs. Dent regarded her with eyes full of the strangest mixture of fear and horror and hostility.

"What do you mean talking so?" she said in a hard voice.

"It *is there*."

"Nonsense. You threw it down and it fell that way."

"It was folded in my bureau drawer."

"It couldn't have been."

"Who picked that red rose?"

"Look on the bush," Mrs. Dent replied shortly.

Rebecca looked at her; her mouth gaped. She hurried out of the room. When she came back her eyes seemed to protrude. (She had in the meantime hastened upstairs, and come down with tottering steps, clinging to the banister.)

"Now I want to know what all this means?" she demanded.

"What what means?"

"The rose is on the bush, and it's gone from the bed in my room! Is this house haunted, or what?"

"I don't know anything about a house being haunted. I don't believe in such things. Be you crazy?" Mrs. Dent spoke with gathering force. The color flashed back to her cheeks.

"No," said Rebecca, shortly, "I ain't crazy yet, but I shall be if this keeps on much longer. I'm going to find out where that girl is before night."

Mrs. Dent eyed her.

"What be you going to do?"

"I'm going to Lincoln."

A faint triumphant smile overspread Mrs. Dent's large face.

"You can't," said she; "there ain't any train."

"No train?"

"No; there ain't any afternoon train from the Falls to Lincoln."

"Then I'm going over to the Slocums' again to-night."

However, Rebecca did not go; such a rain came up as deterred even her resolution, and she had only her best dresses with her. Then in the evening came the letter from the Michigan village which she had left nearly a week ago. It was from her cousin, a single woman, who had come to keep her house while she was away. It was a pleasant unexciting letter enough, all the first of it, and related mostly how she missed Rebecca; how she hoped she was having pleasant weather and kept her health; and how her friend, Mrs. Greenaway, had come to stay with her since she had felt lonesome the first night in the house; how she hoped Rebecca would have no objections to this, although nothing had been said about it, since she had not realized that she might be nervous alone. The cousin was painfully conscientious, hence the letter. Rebecca smiled in spite of her disturbed mind as she read it; then her eye caught the postscript. That was in a different hand, purporting to be written by the friend, Mrs. Hannah Greenaway, informing her that the cousin had fallen down the cellar stairs and broken her hip, and was in a dangerous condition, and begging Rebecca to return at once, as she herself was rheumatic and unable to nurse her properly, and no one else could be obtained.

Rebecca looked at Mrs. Dent, who had come to her room with the letter quite late; it was half-past nine, and she had gone upstairs for the night.

"Where did this come from?" she asked.

"Mr. Amblecrom brought it," she replied.

"Who's he?"

"The postmaster. He often brings the letters that come on the late mail. He knows I ain't anybody to send. He brought yours about your coming. He said he and his wife came over on the ferry-boat with you."

"I remember him," Rebecca replied, shortly. "There bad news in this letter."

Mrs. Dent's face took on an expression of serious inquiry.

"Yes, my Cousin Harriet has fallen down the cellar stairs—they were always dangerous—and she's broken her hip, and I've got to take the first train home to-morrow."

"You don't say so. I'm dreadfully sorry."

"No, you ain't sorry!" said Rebecca with a look as if she leaped. "You're glad. I don't know why, but you're glad. You've wanted to get rid of me for some reason ever since I came. I don't know why. You're a strange woman. Now you've got your way, and I hope you're satisfied."

"How you talk."

Mrs. Dent spoke in a faintly injured voice, but there was a light in her eyes.

"I talk the way it is. Well, I'm going to-morrow morning, and I want you, just as soon as Agnes Dent comes home, to send her out to me. Don't you wait for anything. You pack what clothes she's got, and don't wait even to mend them, and you buy her ticket. I'll leave the money, and you send her along. She don't have to change cars. You start her off, when she gets home, on the next train!"

"Very well," replied the other woman. She had an expression of covert amusement.

"Mind you do it."

"Very well, Rebecca."

Rebecca started on her journey the next morning. When she arrived, two days later, she found her cousin in perfect health. She found, moreover, that the friend had not written the postscript in the cousin's letter. Rebecca would have returned to Ford Village the next morning, but the fatigue and nervous strain had been too much for her. She was not able to move from her bed. She had a species of low fever induced by anxiety and fatigue. But she could write, and she did, to the Slocums, and she received no answer. She also wrote to Mrs. Dent; she even sent numerous telegrams, with no response. Finally she wrote to the postmaster, and an answer arrived by the first possible mail. The letter was short, curt, and to the purpose. Mr. Amblecrom, the postmaster, was a man of few words, and especially wary as to his expressions in a letter.

Dear madam, he wrote,

your favour rec'ed. No Slocums in Ford's Village. All dead. Addie ten years ago, her mother two years later, her father five. House vacant. Mrs. John Dent said to have neglected stepdaughter. Girl was sick. Medicine not given. Talk of taking action. Not enough evidence. House said to be haunted. Strange sights and sounds. Your niece, Agnes Dent, died a year ago, about this time.

> *Yours truly,*
> *Thomas Amblecrom.*

Blow Up
with the Brig!

On the word of a man, it makes my flesh creep now,
only to tell you what he did with me.

I have got an alarming confession to make. I am
haunted by a Ghost.

If you were to guess for a hundred years, you would
never guess what my ghost is. I shall make you laugh
to begin with—and afterward I shall make your flesh
creep. My Ghost is the ghost of a Bedroom Candlestick.

Yes, a bedroom candlestick and candle, or a flat
candlestick and candle—put it which way you like—
that is what haunts me. I wish it was something pleasanter and more out of the common way; a beautiful
lady, or a mine of gold and silver, or a cellar of wine
and a coach and horses, and such like. But, being what
it is, I must take it for what it is, and make the best of

it; and I shall thank you kindly if you will help me out by doing the same.

I am not a scholar myself, but I make bold to believe that the haunting of any man with anything under the sun begins with the frightening of him. At any rate, the haunting of me with a bedroom candlestick and candle began with the frightening of me with a bedroom candlestick and candle—the frightening of me half out of my life; and, for the time being, the frightening of me altogether out of my wits. That is not a very pleasant thing to confess before stating the particulars; but perhaps you will be the readier to believe that I am not a downright coward, because you find me bold enough to make a clean breast of it already, to my own great disadvantage so far.

Here are the particulars, as well as I can put them:

I was apprenticed to the sea when I was about as tall as my own walking-stick; and I made good enough use of my time to be fit for a mate's berth at the age of twenty-five years.

It was in the year eighteen hundred and eighteen, or nineteen, I am not quite certain which, that I reached the before-mentioned age of twenty-five. You will please to excuse my memory not being very good for dates, names, numbers, places, and such like. No fear, though, about the particulars I have undertaken to tell you of; I have got them all shipshape in my recollection; I can see them, at this moment, as clear as noonday in my own mind. But there is a mist over what went before, and, for the matter of that, a mist likewise over much that came after—and it's not very likely to lift at my time of life, is it?

Well, in eighteen hundred and eighteen, or nineteen, when there was peace in our part of the world—and not before it was wanted, you will say—there was fighting, of a certain scampering, scrambling kind, going on in that old battle-field which we sea-faring men know by the name of the Spanish Main.

The possessions that belonged to the Spaniards in South America had broken into open mutiny and declared for themselves years before. There was plenty of bloodshed between the new Government and the old; but the new had got the best of it, for the most part, under one General Bolívar—a famous man in his time, though he seems to have dropped out of people's memories now. Englishmen and Irishmen with a turn for fighting, and nothing particular to do at home, joined the general as volunteers; and some of our merchants here found it a good venture to send supplies across the ocean to the popular side. There was risk enough, of course, in doing this; but where one speculation of the kind succeeded, it made up for two, at the least, that failed. And that's the true principle of trade, wherever I have met with it, all the world over.

Among the Englishmen who were concerned in this Spanish-American business, I, your humble servant, happened, in a small way, to be one.

I was then mate of a brig belonging to a certain firm in the City, which drove a sort of general trade, mostly in queer out-of-the-way places, as far from home as possible; and which freighted the brig, in the year I am speaking of, with a cargo of gunpowder for General Bolívar and his volunteers. Nobody knew anything about our instructions, when we sailed, except the captain; and he didn't half seem to like them. I can't rightly say how many barrels of powder we had on board, or how much each barrel held—I only know we had no other cargo. The name of the brig was the *Good Intent*—a queer name enough, you will tell me, for a vessel laden with gunpowder, and sent to help a revolution. And as far as this particular voyage was concerned, so it was. I mean that for a joke, and I hope you will encourage me by laughing at it.

The *Good Intent* was the craziest tub of a vessel I ever went to sea in, and the worst found in all respects. She was two hundred and thirty or two hundred and eighty tons burden, I forget which; and she had a crew of eight, all told—nothing like as many as we ought by rights to have had to work the brig. However, we were well and honestly paid our wages; and we had to set that against the chance of foundering at sea, and, on this occasion, likewise the chance of being blown up into the bargain.

In consideration of the nature of our cargo, we were harassed with new regulations, which we didn't at all like, relative to smoking our pipes and lighting our lanterns; and, as usual in such cases, the captain, who made the regulations, preached what he didn't practise. Not a man of us was allowed to have a bit of lighted candle in his hand when he went below—except the skipper; and he used his light, when he turned in, or when he looked over his charts on the cabin table, just as usual.

This light was a common kitchen candle or "dip," and it stood in an old battered flat candlestick, with all the japan worn and melted off, and all the tin showing through. It would have been more seaman-like and suitable in every respect if he had had a lamp or a lantern; but he stuck to his old candlestick; and that same old candlestick has ever afterward stuck to *me*.

That's another joke, if you please, and a better one than the first, in my opinion.

Well (I said "well" before, but it's a word that helps a man on like), we sailed in the brig, and shaped our course, first, for the Virgin Islands, in the West Indies; and, after sighting them, we made for the Leeward Islands next, and then stood on due south, till the lookout at the masthead hailed the deck and said he saw land. That land was the coast of South America. We had had a wonderful voyage so far. We had lost none of our spars or sails, and not a man of us had been harassed to death at the pumps. It wasn't often the *Good Intent* made such a voyage as that, I can tell you.

I was sent aloft to make sure about the land, and I did make sure of it.

When I reported the same to the skipper, he went below, and had a look at his letter of instructions and the chart. When he came on deck again, he altered our course a trifle to the eastward—I forget the point on the compass, but that don't matter. What I do remember is, that it was dark before we closed in with the land. We kept the lead going, and hove the brig to in from four to five fathoms water, or it might be six—I can't say for certain. I kept a sharp eye to the drift of the vessel, none of us knowing how the currents ran on that coast. We all wondered why the skipper didn't anchor; but he said No, he must first show a light at the foretopmast-head, and wait for an answering light on shore. We did wait, and nothing of the sort appeared. It was starlight and calm. What little wind there was came in puffs off the land. I suppose we waited, drifting a little to the westward, as I made it

out, best part of an hour before anything happened—
and then, instead of seeing the light on shore, we saw
a boat coming toward us, rowed by two men only.

We hailed them, and they answered "Friends!" and
hailed us by our name. They came on board. One of
them was an Irishman, and the other was a coffee-
coloured native pilot, who jabbered a little English.

The Irishman handed a note to our skipper, who
showed it to me. It informed us that the part of the
coast we were off was not oversafe for discharging our
cargo, seeing that spies of the enemy (that is to say,
of the old Government) had been taken and shot in
the neighbourhood the day before. We might trust the
brig to the native pilot; and he had his instructions to
take us to another part of the coast. The note was
signed by the proper parties; so we let the Irishman
go back alone in the boat, and allowed the pilot to
exercise his lawful authority over the brig. He kept us
stretching off from the land till noon the next day—
his instructions, seemingly, ordering him to keep up
well out of sight of the shore. We only altered our
course in the afternoon, so as to close in with the land
again a little before midnight.

This same pilot was about as ill-looking a vagabond
as ever I saw; a skinny, cowardly, quarrelsome mon-
grel, who swore at the men in the vilest broken English, till they were every one of them ready to pitch
him overboard. The skipper kept them quiet, and I
kept them quiet; for the pilot being given us by our
instructions, we were bound to make the best of him.
Near night-fall, however, with the best will in the
world to avoid it, I was unlucky enough to quarrel
with him.

He wanted to go below with his pipe, and I stopped

him, of course, because it was contrary to orders. Upon that he tried to hustle by me, and I put him away with my hand. I never meant to push him down; but somehow I did. He picked himself up as quick as lightning, and pulled out his knife. I snatched it out of his hand, slapped his murderous face for him, and threw his weapon overboard. He gave me one ugly look, and walked aft. I didn't think much of the look then, but I remembered it a little too well afterward.

We were close in with the land again, just as the wind failed us, between eleven and twelve that night, and dropped our anchor by the pilot's directions.

It was pitch-dark, and a dead, airless calm. The skipper was on deck, with two of our best men for watch. The rest were below, except the pilot, who coiled himself up, more like a snake than a man, on the forecastle. It was not my watch till four in the morning. But I didn't like the look of the night, or the pilot, or the state of things generally, and I shook myself down on deck to get my nap there, and be ready for anything at a moment's notice. The last I remember was the skipper whispering to me that he didn't like the look of things either, and that he would go below and consult his instructions again. That is the last I remember, before the slow, heavy, regular roll of the old brig on the groundswell rocked me off to sleep.

I was awoke by a scuffle on the forecastle and a gag in my mouth. There was a man on my breast and a man on my legs, and I was bound hand and foot in half a minute.

The brig was in the hands of the Spaniards. They were swarming all over her. I heard six heavy splashes in the water, one after another. I saw the captain stabbed to the heart as he came running up the companion, and I heard a seventh splash in the water. Except myself, every soul of us on board had been murdered and thrown into the sea. Why I was left, I couldn't think, till I saw the pilot stoop over me with a lantern and look, to make sure of who I was. There was a devilish grin on his face, and he nodded his head at me, as much as to say, *You* were the man who hustled me down and slapped my face, and I mean to play the game of cat and mouse with you in return for it!

I could neither move nor speak, but I could see the Spaniards take off the main hatch and rig the purchases for getting up the cargo. A quarter of an hour afterward I heard the sweeps of a schooner, or other small vessel, in the water. The strange craft was laid alongside of us, and the Spaniards set to work to discharge our cargo into her. They all worked hard except the pilot; and he came from time to time, with his lantern, to have another look at me, and to grin and nod always in the same devilish way. I am old enough now not to be ashamed of confessing the truth, and I don't mind acknowledging that the pilot frightened me.

The fright, and the bonds, and the gag, and the not being able to stir hand or foot, had pretty nigh worn me out by the time the Spaniards gave over work. This was just as the dawn broke. They had shifted a good part of our cargo on board their vessel, but nothing like all of it, and they were sharp enough to be off with what they had got before daylight.

I need hardly say that I had made up my mind by this time to the worst I could think of. The pilot, it was clear enough, was one of the spies of the enemy, who

had wormed himself into the confidence of our con-
signees without being suspected. He, or more likely his
employers, had got knowledge enough of us to suspect
what our cargo was; we had been anchored for the
night in the safest berth for them to surprise us in;
and we had paid the penalty of having a small crew,
and consequently an insufficient watch. All this was
clear enough—but what did the pilot mean to do
with *me?*

On the word of a man, it makes my flesh creep now,
only to tell you what he did with me.

After all the rest of them were out of the brig, except the pilot and two Spanish seamen, these last took
me up, bound and gagged as I was, lowered me into
the hold of the vessel, and laid me along on the floor,
lashing me to it with ropes' ends, so that I could just
turn from one side to the other, but could not roll myself fairly over, so as to change my place. They then
left me. Both of them were the worse for liquor; but
the devil of a pilot was sober—mind that!—as sober
as I am at the present moment.

I lay in the dark for a little while, with my heart
thumping as if it was going to jump out of me. I lay
about five minutes or so when the pilot came down
into the hold alone.

He had the captain's cursed flat candlestick and a
carpenter's awl in one hand, and a long thin twist of
cotton-yard, well oiled, in the other. He put the candlestick, with a new "dip" candle lighted in it, down
on the floor about two feet from my face, and close
against the side of the vessel. The light was feeble
enough; but it was sufficient to show a dozen barrels of
gunpowder or more left all round me in the hold of
the brig. I began to suspect what he was after the

moment I noticed the barrels. The horrors laid hold of me from head to foot, and the sweat poured off my face like water.

I saw him go next to one of the barrels of powder standing against the side of the vessel in a line with the candle, and about three feet, or rather better, away from it. He bored a hole in the side of the barrel with his awl, and the horrid powder came trickling out, as black as hell, and dripped into the hollow of his hand, which he held to catch it. When he had got a good handful, he stopped up the hole by jamming one end of his oiled twist of cotton-yarn fast into it, and he then rubbed the powder into the whole length of the yarn till he had blackened every hair-breadth of it.

The next thing he did—as true as I sit here, as true as the heaven above us all—the next thing he did was to carry the free end of his long, lean, black, frightful slow-match to the lighted candle alongside my face. He tied it (the bloody-minded villain!) in several folds round the tallow dip, about a third of the distance down, measuring from the flame of the wick to the lip of the candlestick. He did that; he looked to see that my lashings were all safe; and then he put his face close to mine, and whispered in my ear, "Blow up with the brig!"

He was on deck again the moment after, and he and the two others shoved the hatch on over me. At the farthest end from where I lay they had not fitted it down quite true, and I saw a blink of daylight glimmering in when I looked in that direction. I heard the sweeps of the schooner fall into the water—splash! splash! fainter and fainter, as they swept the vessel out in the dead calm, to be ready for the wind in the offing. Fainter and fainter, splash, splash! For a quarter of an hour or more.

While those receding sounds were in my ears, my eyes were fixed on the candle.

It had been freshly lighted. If left to itself, it would burn for between six and seven hours. The slow-match was twisted round it about a third of the way down, and therefore the flame would be about two hours reaching it. There I lay, gagged, bound, lashed to the floor; seeing my own life burning down with the candle by my side—there I lay, alone on the sea, doomed to be blown to atoms, and to see that doom drawing on, nearer and nearer with every fresh second of time, through nigh on two hours to come; powerless to help myself, and speechless to call for help to others. The wonder to me is that I didn't cheat the flame, the slow-match, and the powder, and die of the horror of my situation before my first half-hour was out in the hold of the brig.

I can't exactly say how long I kept the command of my senses after I had ceased to hear the splash of the schooner's sweeps in the water. I can trace back everything I did and everything I thought, up to a certain point; but, once past that, I get all abroad, and lose myself in my memory now, much as I lost myself in my own feelings at the time.

The moment the hatch was covered over me, I began, as every other man would have begun in my place, with a frantic effort to free my hands. In the mad panic I was in, I cut my flesh with the lashings as if they had been knife-blades, but I never stirred them. There was less chance still of freeing my legs, or of tearing myself from the fastenings that held me to the floor. I gave in when I was all but suffocated for want of breath. The gag, you will please to remember, was a terrible enemy to me; I could only breathe freely through my nose— and that is but a poor vent when a man is straining his strength as far as ever it will go.

I gave in and lay quiet, and got my breath again, my eyes glaring and straining at the candle all the time.

While I was staring at it, the notion struck me of trying to blow out the flame by pumping a long breath at it suddenly through my nostrils. It was too high above me, and too far away from me, to be reached in that fashion. I tried, and tried, and tried; and then I gave in again, and lay quiet again, always with my eyes glaring at the candle, and the candle glaring at *me*. The splash of the schooner's sweeps was very faint by this time. I could only just hear them in the morning stillness. Splash! splash!—fainter and fainter— splash! splash!

Without exactly feeling my mind going, I began to feel it getting queer as early as this. The snuff of the candle was growing taller and taller, and the length of tallow between the flame and the slow-match, which was the length of my life, was getting shorter and shorter. I calculated that I had rather less than an hour and a half to live.

An hour and a half! Was there a chance in that time of a boat pulling off to the brig from shore? Whether the land near which the vessel was anchored was in possession of our side, or in possession of the enemy's side, I made out that they must, sooner or later, send to hail the brig merely because she was a stranger in those parts. The question for *me* was, how soon? The sun had not risen yet, as I could tell by looking through the chink in the hatch. There was no coast village near us, as we all knew, before the brig was seized, by seeing no lights on shore. There was no wind, as I could tell by listening, to bring any strange vessel near. If I had had six hours to live, there might have been a chance for me, reckoning from sunrise to noon. But with an hour and a half, which had dwindled to an hour and a quarter by this time—or, in other words, with the earliness of the morning, the uninhabited coast, and the dead calm all against me—there was not the ghost of a chance. As I felt that, I had another struggle—the last—with my bonds, and only cut myself the deeper for my pains.

I gave in once more, and lay quiet, and listened for the splash of the sweeps.

Gone! Not a sound could I hear but the blowing of a fish now and then on the surface of the sea, and the creak of the brig's crazy old spars, as she rolled gently from side to side with the little swell there was on the quiet water.

An hour and a quarter. The wick grew terribly as the quarter slipped away, and the charred top of it began to thicken and spread out mushroom-shape. It would fall off soon. Would it fall off red-hot, and would the swing of the brig cant it over the side of the candle and let it down on the slow-match? If it would, I had about ten minutes to live instead of an hour.

This discovery set my mind for a minute on a new tack altogether. I began to ponder with myself what sort of a death blowing up might be. Painful! Well, it would be, surely, too sudden for that. Perhaps just one crash inside me, or outside me, or both; and nothing more! Perhaps not even a crash; that and death and the scattering of this living body of mine into millions of fiery sparks, might all happen in the same instant! I couldn't make it out; I couldn't settle how it would be. The minute of calmness in my mind left it before I had half done thinking; and I got all abroad again.

When I came back to my thoughts, or when they came back to me (I can't say which), the wick was awfully tall, the flame was burning with a smoke above it, the charred top was broad and red, and heavily spreading out to its fall.

My despair and horror at seeing it took me in a new way, which was good and right, at any rate, for my poor soul. I tried to pray—in my own heart, you will understand, for the gag put all lip-praying out of my power. I tried, but the candle seemed to burn it up in me. I struggled hard to force my eyes from the slow, murdering flame, and to look up through the chink in the hatch at the blessed daylight. I tried once, tried twice; and gave it up. I next tried only to shut my eyes, and keep them shut—once—twice—and the second time I did it. "God bless old mother, and sister Lizzie; God keep them both, and forgive *me*." That was all I had time to say, in my own heart, before my eyes opened again, in spite of me, and the flame of the candle flew into them, flew all over me, and burned up the rest of my thoughts in an instant.

I couldn't hear the fish blowing now; I couldn't hear the creak of the spars; I couldn't think; I couldn't feel the sweat of my own death agony on my face—I could only look at the heavy, charred top of the wick. It swelled, tottered, bent over to one side, dropped—red-hot at the moment of its fall—black and harmless, even before the swing of the brig had canted it over into the bottom of the candlestick.

I caught myself laughing.

Yes! laughing at the safe fall of the bit of wick. But for the gag, I should have screamed with laughing. As it was, I shook with it inside me—shook till the blood was in my head, and I was all but suffocated for want of breath. I had just sense enough left to feel that my own horrid laughter at that awful moment was a sign of my brain going at last. I had just sense enough left to make another struggle before my mind broke loose like a frightened horse, and ran away with me.

One comforting look at the blink of daylight through the hatch was what I tried for once more. The fight to force my eyes from the candle and to get that one look at the daylight was the hardest I had had yet; and I lost the fight. The flame had hold of my eyes as fast as the lashings had hold of my hands. I couldn't look away from it. I couldn't even shut my eyes, when I tried that next, for the second time. There was the wick growing tall once more. There was the space of unburned candle between the light and the slow-match shortened to an inch or less.

How much life did that inch leave me? Three-quarters of an hour? Half an hour? Fifty minutes? Twenty minutes? Steady! an inch of tallow-candle would burn longer than twenty minutes. An inch of tallow! the notion of a man's body and soul being kept together by an inch of tallow! Wonderful! Why, the greatest king that sits on a throne can't keep a man's body and soul together; and here's an inch of tallow that can do what the king can't! There's something to tell mother when I get home which will sur-

prise her more than all the rest of my voyages put together. I laughed inwardly again at the thought of
that, and shook and swelled and suffocated myself, till
the light of the candle leaped in through my eyes, and
licked up the laughter, and burned it out of me, and
made me all empty and cold and quiet once more.

Mother and Lizzie. I don't know when they came
back; but they did come back—not, as it seemed to me,
into my mind this time, but right down bodily before
me, in the hold of the brig.

Yes: sure enough, there was Lizzie, just as light-
hearted as usual, laughing at me. Laughing? Well,
why not? Who is to blame Lizzie for thinking I'm lying on my back, drunk in the cellar, with the beer-
barrels all round me? Steady! she's crying now—
spinning round and round in a fiery mist, wringing her
hands, screeching out for help—fainter and fainter,
like the splash of the schooner's sweeps. Gone—
burned up in the fiery mist! Mist? fire? no; neither one
nor the other. It's mother makes the light—mother
knitting, with ten flaming points at the ends of her
fingers and thumbs, and slow-matches hanging in
bunches all round her face instead of her own grey
hair. Mother in her old arm-chair, and the pilot's long
skinny hands hanging over the back of the chair, dripping with gunpowder. No! no gunpowder, no chair, no
mother—nothing but the pilot's face, shining red-hot,
like a sun, in the fiery mist; turning upside down in the
fiery mist; running backward and forward along the
slow-match, in the fiery mist; spinning millions of miles
in a minute, in the fiery mist—spinning itself smaller
and smaller into one tiny point, and that point darting
on a sudden straight into my head—and then, all fire
and all mist—no hearing, no seeing, no thinking, no

feeling—the brig, the sea, my own self, the whole world, all gone together!

After what I've just told you, I know nothing and remember nothing, till I woke up (as it seemed to me) in a comfortable bed, with two rough-and-ready men like myself sitting on each side of my pillow, and a gentleman standing watching me at the foot of the bed. It was about seven in the morning. My sleep (or what seemed like my sleep to me) had lasted better than eight months—I was among my own countrymen in the island of Trinidad—the men at each side of my pillow were my keepers, turn and turn about—and the gentleman standing at the foot of the bed was the doctor. What I said and did in those eight months, I never have known, and never shall. I woke out of it as if it had been one long sleep—that's all I know.

It was another two months or more before the doctor thought it safe to answer the questions I asked him.

The brig had been anchored, just as I had supposed, off a part of the coast which was lonely enough to make the Spaniards pretty sure of no interruption, so long as they managed their murderous work quietly under cover of night.

My life had not been saved from the shore, but from the sea. An American vessel, becalmed in the offing, had made out the brig as the sun rose; and the captain having his time on his hands in consequence of the calm, and seeing a vessel anchored where no vessel had any reason to be, had manned one of his boats and sent his mate with it, to look a little closer into the matter, and bring back a report of what he saw.

What he saw, when he and his men found the brig deserted and boarded her, was a gleam of candle-light through the chink in the hatchway. The flame was within about a thread's breadth of the slow-match when he lowered himself into the hold; and if he had not had the sense and coolness to cut the match in two with his knife before he touched the candle, he and his men might have been blown up along with the brig as well as me. The match caught, and turned into sputtering red fire, in the very act of putting the candle out; and if the communication with the powder-barrel had not been cut off, the Lord only knows what might have happened.

What became of the Spanish schooner and the pilot, I have never heard from that day to this.

As for the brig, the Yankees took her, as they took me, to Trinidad, and claimed their salvage, and got it, I hope, for their own sakes. I was landed just in the same state as when they rescued me from the brig—that is to say, clean out of my senses. But please to remember, it was a long time ago; and, take my word for it, I was discharged cured, as I have told you. Bless your hearts, I'm all right now, as you may see. I'm a little shaken by telling the story, as is only natural—a little shaken, my good friends, that's all.

The Web

*The boy fell back in amazement at the alarm and panic
in his grandfather.*

The old man was sitting in the drawing room, still and
calm like a sculptor's model, the sun splashing weakly
on his legs; and the boy came in from school, the red
of the romp in his cheeks and his eyes bright.

"That you, Joe?"

"Hi, Gramp."

They had known each other a week. The old man
was still strange in the house, but he had encompassed
the family, his daughter, her husband, both except the
boy. The boy seemed to be walking around the outskirts of his friendliness, now and then edging over the
line, but scuttling back again. He sensed about him a
manner he could not fathom.

Now the boy threw his schoolbag down, went to the
sideboard and picked up an apple. Slowly, he tiptoed
towards his grandfather, cautiously moved all around

him, taking in the big-boned frame, and warily moving to the front and staring at the serene blue eyes; staring.

He felt the impact of incomprehension; the incredulity of eyes that were eyes in every way, that looked at him and yet could not see him; and he knew in his own way the inertness of that mass that was yet alive; the helplessness. It horrified him.

"Have a good day at school, son?"

"Okay. Got the cuts for fightin', but."

He saw the old man's mouth break open, while the expression of the eyes remained unaltered; and he saw on that part of the face under the eyes a curious vivacity of amusement.

Suddenly the boy's eyes shifted, his neck craned forward, and he said: "Don't move, Gramp. There's a spider on your arm."

He might have told the old man there was a stick of dynamite at his feet, for he was electrified into movement, while horror jumped on to his face, and he struggled forward in his chair, brushing his clothes wildly and blindly, and crying: "Get it off me! Get it off me!"

The boy fell back in amazement at the alarm and panic in his grandfather. Then he bustled up to him and said: "Keep still, and I'll get him. He's on your leg now. He's only a little one." He slapped at the man's thigh and brushed the spider to the carpet, grinding it with his boot and making sounds of emphasis with his mouth.

"There, he's dead now. I got him."

He saw the old man collapse in his chair, panting, his face chalky, and his hands shaking; trying to speak.

"I hate them things," he muttered huskily.

"Well, he's dead now. I squashed him."

"Good boy, Joe." There was relief and pleasure in the old man's voice. He fumbled in his pocket, and the boy's face lit greedily at the jingle of coins. "Here. Here's thrippence. You go and buy some lollies. That's the boy."

The boy took the money and backed away, delighted, but still astonished at the change that had come over his grandfather.

A week later the boy with two of his schoolmates came up to the old man sitting in the back yard, and said: "Gramp, did you ever eat aniseed balls?"

"Years ago."

"Did you like them?" asked the boy eagerly.

"I certainly did."

"Well, I know where I can get some, Gramp. Down at the corner shop. They're all in the window. Would you like me to get you some?"

The old man put his hand in his pocket, and with a chuckle handed the boy sixpence. "You get some for you and your pals, Joe; I'll have some another day."

"Gee, thanks, Gramp."

That evening the old man's daughter said to him: "You mustn't be giving money to Joe."

"Only sixpence," he said.

"I don't want you to do it, Father. He gets enough pocket-money without bothering you. And besides, I don't want him to be filling himself up with gut-rot all the time. Please don't give him any more."

"All right," he said. He knew the tone of her voice, and he was a prisoner of their stewardship. But he didn't mind giving the boy money. It was helping to bridge the gulf between them, coaxing the boy into fearless friendship, subtly easing away whatever strangeness it was that kept him vaguely remote.

When the boy asked again the old man refused him. The boy tried all sorts of subterfuges, but his grandfather would not relent. He told him he was short of change, or gave some other excuse. The boy was broodingly bitter. He had wanted the money especially. He was desperate in his rage, furious because he had suffered a knockback at what he had come to take for granted, and because there was no other source of extra income open to him.

"Mingy old cow," he said with hate.

He affected not to hold any animosity. He had his scheme worked out. He tried it one day when his mother and father were out, and he was alone with the old man in the house.

He suddenly chirruped excitedly: "Oh look, Gramp, there's another spider."

"Where? Where?" cried the old man, disturbance shaking him again.

"It's not near you. It's on the table."

"Kill it, then. Kill it. Don't let it come near me."

"But it won't touch you, Gramp. It's on the table, I said."

The old man was stumbling out of his chair, the sweat on his face. He sat still for a second, panting.

"Oh, it's moving across the table now. It's moving. Can spiders smell you, Gramp?"

"Kill it!" screamed the old man. "Kill it before it drops to the floor."

The boy watched with hypnotic delight, sensing the power that he wielded: this huge old man subject to him.

58

"What'll you give me if I kill it?" he breathed.

"Anything, anything. Where is it now?"

"Sixpence?"

"Yes, yes."

The boy made a slapping sound. Then he breathed with triumph. "Now it'll never get you, Gramp. Gimme the sixpence that you said you would. Oh, it's not quite dead. Gimme the sixpence, Gramp, and I'll squash it with the sixpence."

The old man's money jingled and split in a jingle out of his hand. The boy gathered up the coins. He put sixpence in his pocket. Then he held out the money, and tipped it into the man's hand. The man searched with his fingers, and gave the boy sixpence.

"Thanks, Gramp. Gee, he was a big spider, too. Brown. Hairy legs."

"Don't tell me about it!" yelled the old man. "I don't want to hear about it. Get out of here. Are you sure you killed it?"

"Oh yes, Gramp. It's all squashed up. You can feel it here."

"No, no. Get it away from me."

The boy's lips eased apart over his sharp little teeth, and his hand was on the two sixpences in his pocket.

"Crikey, Gramp, I don't know what makes you so scared of spiders."

"I hate 'em. I hated 'em all my life. I killed every one I saw. There's a lot of spiders in this house."

"But you needn't worry, Gramp. I'll kill every spider I see, and I'll kill 'em just for you, and you needn't gimme any more than a penny if you don't want to."

The old man's breathing came stiffly. He waved a hand: "All right. All right. Leave me alone now. And don't tell your mother I gave you that sixpence."

"No fear, Gramp. It's just a secret between you and me."

He raced out joyfully.

The boy was very cunning. He didn't try again for a fortnight. And in the meantime, when he was sitting outside one day with the old man, the old man said: "You don't dislike spiders, do you, Joey?"

"No, Gramp," the boy said ingenuously.

"I hate 'em," the old man said emphatically.

The boy got away with it once more. He waited until the old man was well on in his pitiable terror. Then he played for the stakes.

"Will you gimme a shilling if I kill it?"

As soon as he had said it, he noticed a sudden change in the old man; it was only momentarily, but he noticed it. The old man, still gripped in terror, only nodded.

"Gimme the shilling first, then," the boy said warily.

When he had it he made a great business of killing the imaginary redback; and he talked a lot, but the old man said nothing. He tried to get some assurance from the old man that he was a good boy, and had made the old man happy by killing the spider. But all he got was silence. He went away worried, yet defiant and joyous.

When he tried again, the old man's lips came together, and a great anger shook him: "You dirty little blackmailer. Get out of my sight. Get out, or I'll tell your mother what sort of a son she's got. Get out!" he yelled. And the boy ran frightened at the wrath in him, but his blood on fire with hate.

The old man shook not with fear, but with a nervous emotion of unpleasantness. Now he had driven the boy like a wild cat beyond the confines of his friendship. He had alienated him. Soon he began to sense the boy's loss about him, and that loss gave the silence chimeras which had never been there before. He began to see spiders as if the boy were pointing them out to him.

In his sleep at night it was not with the terror of an explosion that he awoke. The nightmare descent of dusty darkness and wheels of light spinning in his brain; and noises that were rescuers; and the fresh air meeting his face after the foul stink of the mine; and the great palling abyss of non-independence that had enclosed him until the words of his daughter in his ear gave him knowledge of security and care—four walls and a roof and a watcher.

That was terrible enough, but it was horror that woke him raving; drenched in sweat, crazily slapping at the bed-clothes, at the thousand crawling things on his flesh; and spitting out the spiders that crawled down his throat, their bulbous eyes seeking, and their hairy legs spiking his tongue. It was spiders, hundreds of thousands of them, creeping out of the darkness— the real ghosts of his sleep.

And there was one that came, standing on the floor; its body above the bed, black as tar and yellow-streaked, the hair bristling on it, its leg joints like fractured sticks, its eyes as big as oranges and its mouth scarlet. And swiftly it worked, netting the bed in silken cables, enmeshing him. He sobbed and ranted against it; and only a woman's voice full of agitation could assure him that it was driven away, and was no part, had never been a part, of that other darkness.

The old man tried to get on with the boy, speaking kindly to him, coaxing and cajoling, but he couldn't. Yet the boy did not worry him for weeks. He was thus not prepared for the incident when it did happen. He was sitting in the drawing room again, the sun through the window warming his legs. He was dozing. The

boy, with a companion, sneaked into the porch, tiptoed to the door and looked in.

He put a finger to his lips and said in a whisper:
"You watch."

Then he said in alarm: "Oh, Grandpa, Grandpa,
look! There's a spider!"

The old man started up, jabbering. Then his face
darkened, and he cried out to the boy to get away.

"But, Gramp, it's true. It's true," piped the boy
shrilly.

"You little devil, get when I tell you!"

"All right, don't believe me. He's on your knee!
He's on your knee!"

The old man's mouth opened. Perhaps the boy was
right. He slapped at his knee, the panic working up
in him, the shock and terror paralysing and activating
him.

Then he cried: "You lying hound! God, if I only
had my eyes."

The boy grinned at his companion, who grinned
back. Then he took a matchbox from his pocket, and
edging closer to the agitated old man, opened the
box and dropped the half-stunned spider on his hand,
at the same time stepping back quickly and yelling:
"He's on your hand! Look out!"

The old man pulled his hand away with a ghastly
expression on his face, and terror gurgling in his voice,
and he smashed with his hands, squashing the spider
against his knee, and then in a frenzy slapping it off,
and rising to his feet, choking and sobbing, groping
and blundering.

Then he heard the snickering titter of the boy, and
the echo of it from the other, and he knew he was the
dupe of a cruel joke; it went like a storm through him,

and his hand closed on his walking stick; he went berserk, a scream of fury bursting from his iron lungs, as he swished blindly, the cane singing through space.

The boy fell back in fright as though caught in the vestiges of a tornado. His companion at the door bolted. The old man slashed and the sound of a globe shattered about his ears; glass and wood crashed and tinkled; and the boy's affrighted cries blabbed his whereabouts, pinpointed the target. He was screaming, darting behind chairs, under the table; the cane met his shoulder and cracked against his head, and cracked, and he fell with a sob, fell and crawled towards the door, bloody and stunned to a silence; and sat huddled on the threshold.

And then the old man, aware of the silence, stopped his swishing. He stood upright, gaping in horror. He dropped the cane from his nerveless fingers and cried out in a distracted voice: "Joe! Joe!"

The silence shouted back, and it put him on the floor in a craze of fear, down on his hands and knees, groping and crawling, shrieking: "Joe! Joe! Where are you, Joe?"

And the boy, numb with shock, watching him from the door, began to cry deeply with the outrageous self-pity of his experience.

———◆———

To Build a Fire

*He had felt the give under his feet and heard the
crackle of a snow-hidden ice-skin.*

Day had broken cold and grey, exceedingly cold and
grey, when the man turned aside from the main Yukon
trail and climbed the high earth-bank, where a dim
and little-travelled trail led eastward through the fat
spruce timberland. It was a steep bank, and he paused
for breath at the top, excusing the act to himself by
looking at his watch. It was nine o'clock. There was
no sun nor a hint of sun, though there was not a cloud
in the sky. It was a clear day, and yet there seemed an
intangible pall over the face of things, a subtle gloom
that made the day dark, and that was due to the
absence of sun. This fact did not worry the man. He
was used to the lack of sun. It had been days since
he had seen the sun, and he knew that a few more days
must pass before that cheerful orb, due south, would

just peep about the sky-line and dip immediately from view.

The man flung a look back along the way he had come. The Yukon lay a mile wide and hidden under three feet of ice. On top of this ice were as many feet of snow. It was all pure white, rolling in gentle undulations where the ice-jams of the freeze-up had formed. North and south, as far as his eye could see, it was unbroken white, save for a dark hair-line that curved and twisted from around the spruce-covered island to the south, and that curved and twisted away into the north, where it disappeared behind another spruce-covered island. This dark hair-line was the trail—the main trail—that led south five hundred miles to the Chilkoot Pass, Dyea, and salt water; and that led north seventy miles to Dawson, and still on to the north a thousand miles to Nulato, and finally to St. Michael on Bering Sea, a thousand miles and a half a thousand more.

But all this—the mysterious, far-reaching hair-line trail, the absence of sun from the sky, the tremendous cold, and the strangeness and weirdness of it all— made no impression on the man. It was not because he was long used to it. He was a newcomer in the land, *a chechaquo,* and this was his first winter. The trouble with him was that he was without imagination. He was quick and alert in the things of life, but only in the things, and not in the significances. Fifty degrees below zero meant eighty-odd degrees of frost. Such fact impressed him as being cold and uncomfortable, and that was all. It did not lead him to meditate upon his frailty as a creature of temperature, and upon man's frailty in general, able only to live within certain narrow limits of heat and cold; and from there on it did not lead him to the conjectural field of immortality and man's place in the universe. Fifty degrees below zero stood for a bite of frost that hurt and that must be guarded against by the use of mittens, ear-flaps, warm moccasins, and thick socks. Fifty degrees below zero was to him just precisely fifty degrees below zero. That there should be anything more to it than that was a thought that never entered his head.

As he turned to go on, he spat speculatively. There was a sharp, explosive crackle that startled him. He spat again. And again, in the air, before it could fall to the snow, the spittle crackled. He knew that at fifty below spittle crackled on the snow, but this spittle had crackled in the air. Undoubtedly it was colder than fifty below—how much colder he did not know. But the temperature did not matter. He was bound for the old claim on the left fork of Henderson Creek, where the boys were already. They had come over across the divide from the Indian Creek country, while he had come the roundabout way to take a look at the possibilities of getting out logs in the spring from the islands in the Yukon. He would be in to camp by six o'clock; a bit after dark, it was true, but the boys would be there, a fire would be going, and a hot supper would be ready. As for lunch, he pressed his hand against the protruding bundle under his jacket. It was also under his shirt, wrapped up in a handkerchief and lying against the naked skin. It was the only way to keep the biscuits from freezing. He smiled agreeably to himself as he thought of those biscuits, each cut open and sopped in bacon grease, and each enclosing a generous slice of fried bacon.

He plunged in among the big spruce trees. The trail was faint. A foot of snow had fallen since the last sled had passed over, and he was glad he was without a sled, travelling light. In fact, he carried nothing but the lunch wrapped in the handkerchief. He was surprised, however, at the cold. It certainly was cold, he concluded, as he rubbed his numb nose and cheek-bones with his mittened hand. He was a warm-whiskered man, but the hair on his face did not protect the high cheek-bones and the eager nose that thrust itself aggressively into the frosty air.

At the man's heels trotted a dog, a big native husky, the proper wolf-dog, grey-coated and without any visible or temperamental difference from its brother, the wild wolf. The animal was depressed by the tremendous cold. It knew that it was no time for travelling. Its instinct told it a truer tale than was told to the man by the man's judgment. In reality, it was not merely colder than fifty below zero; it was colder than sixty below, than seventy below. It was seventy-five below zero. Since the freezing-point is thirty-two above zero, it meant that one hundred and seven degrees of frost obtained. The dog did not know anything about thermometers. Possibly in its brain there was no sharp consciousness of a condition of very cold such as was in the man's brain. But the brute had its instincts. It experienced a vague but menacing apprehension that subdued it and made it slink along at the man's heels, and that made it question eagerly every unwonted movement of the man as if expecting him to go into camp or to seek shelter somewhere and build a fire. The dog had learned fire, and it wanted fire, or else to burrow under the snow and cuddle its warmth away from the air.

The frozen moisture of its breathing had settled on its fur in a fine powder of frost, and especially were its jowls, muzzle, and eyelashes whitened by its crystalled breath. The man's red beard and mustache were likewise frosted, but more solidly, the deposit taking the form of ice and increasing with every warm, moist breath he exhaled. Also, the man was chewing tobacco, and the muzzle of ice held his lips so rigidly that he was unable to clear his chin when he expelled the juice. The result was that a crystal beard of the color and solidity of amber was increasing its length on his chin. If he fell down it would shatter itself, like glass, into brittle fragments. But he did not mind the appendage. It was the penalty all tobacco-chewers paid in that country, and he had been out before in two cold snaps. They had not been so cold as this, he knew, but by the spirit thermometer at Sixty Mile he knew they had been registered at fifty below and at fifty-five.

He held on through the level stretch of woods for several miles, crossed a wide flat of nigger-heads, and dropped down a bank to the frozen bed of a small stream. This was Henderson Creek, and he knew he was ten miles from the forks. He looked at his watch. It was ten o'clock. He was making four miles an hour, and he calculated that he would arrive at the forks at half-past twelve. He decided to celebrate that event by eating his lunch there.

The dog dropped in again at his heels, with a tail drooping discouragement, as the man swung along the creek-bed. The furrow of the old sled-trail was plainly visible, but a dozen inches of snow covered the marks of the last runners. In a month no man had come up or down that silent creek. The man held steadily on. He was not much given to thinking, and just then particularly he had nothing to think about save that he would eat lunch at the forks and that at six o'clock he would be in camp with the boys. There was nobody to talk to; and, had there been, speech would have been impossible because of the ice-muzzle on his mouth. So he continued monotonously to chew tobacco and to increase the length of his amber beard.

Once in a while the thought reiterated itself that it was very cold and that he had never experienced such cold. As he walked along he rubbed his cheek-bones and nose with the back of his mittened hand. He did this automatically, now and again changing hands. But rub as he would, the instant he stopped his cheek-bones went numb, and the following instant the end of his nose went numb. He was sure to frost his cheeks; he knew that, and experienced a pang of regret that he had not devised a nose-strap of the sort Bud wore in cold snaps. Such a strap passed across the cheeks, as well, and saved them. But it didn't matter much, after all. What were frosted cheeks? A bit painful, that was all; they were never serious.

Empty as the man's mind was of thoughts, he was keenly observant, and he noticed the changes in the creek, the curves and bends and timber-jams, and always he sharply noted where he placed his feet. Once, coming around a bend, he shied abruptly, like a startled horse, curved away from the place where he had been walking, and retreated several paces back along the trail. The creek he knew was frozen clear to the bottom,—no creek could contain water in that arctic winter,—but he knew also that there were springs that bubbled out from the hillsides and ran along under the snow and on top the ice of the creek. He knew that the coldest snaps never froze these springs, and he knew likewise their danger. They were traps. They hid pools of water under the snow that might be three inches deep, or three feet. Sometimes a skin of ice half an inch thick covered them, and in turn was covered by the snow. Sometimes there were alternate layers of water and ice-skin, so that when one broke through he kept on breaking through for a while, sometimes wetting himself to the waist.

That was why he had shied in such panic. He had felt the give under his feet and heard the crackle of a snow-hidden ice-skin. And to get his feet wet in such a temperature meant trouble and danger. At the very least it meant delay, for he would be forced to stop and build a fire, and under its protection to bare his feet while he dried his socks and moccasins. He stood and studied the creek-bed and its banks, and decided that the flow of water came from the right. He reflected awhile, rubbing his nose and cheeks, then skirted to the left, stepping gingerly and testing the footing for each step. Once clear of the danger, he took a fresh chew of tobacco and swung along at his four-mile gait.

In the course of the next two hours he came upon several similar traps. Usually the snow above the hidden pools had a sunken, candied appearance that advertised the danger. Once again, however, he had a close call; and once, suspecting danger, he compelled the dog to go on in front. The dog did not want to go. It hung back until the man shoved it forward, and then it went quickly across the white, unbroken surface. Suddenly it broke through, floundered to one side, and got away to firmer footing. It had wet its forefeet and legs, and almost immediately the water that clung to it turned to ice. It made quick efforts to lick the ice off its legs, then dropped down in the snow and began to bite out the ice that had formed between the toes.

This was a matter of instinct. To permit the ice to remain would mean sore feet. It did not know this. It merely obeyed the mysterious prompting that arose from the deep crypts of its being. But the man knew, having achieved a judgment on the subject, and he removed the mitten from his right hand and helped tear out the ice-particles. He did not expose his fingers more than a minute, and was astonished at the swift numbness that smote them. It certainly was cold. He pulled on the mitten hastily, and beat the hand savagely across his chest.

At twelve o'clock the day was at its brightest. Yet the sun was too far south on its winter journey to clear the horizon. The bulge of the earth intervened between it and Henderson Creek, where the man walked under a clear sky at noon and cast no shadow. At half-past twelve, to the minute, he arrived at the forks of the creek. He was pleased at the speed he had made. If he kept it up, he would certainly be with the boys by six. He unbuttoned his jacket and shirt and drew forth his lunch. The action consumed no more than a quarter of a minute, yet in that brief moment the numbness laid hold of the exposed fingers. He did not put the mitten on, but, instead, struck the fingers a dozen sharp smashes against his leg. Then he sat down on a snow-covered log to eat. The sting that followed upon the striking of his fingers against his leg ceased so quickly that he was startled. He had had no chance to take a bite of biscuit. He struck the fingers repeatedly and returned them to the mitten, baring the other hand for the purpose of eating. He tried to take a mouthful, but the ice-muzzle prevented. He had forgotten to build a fire and thaw out. He chuckled at his foolishness, and as he chuckled he noted the numbness creeping into the exposed fingers. Also, he noted that the stinging which had first come to his toes when he sat down was already passing away. He wondered whether the toes were warm or numb. He moved them inside the moccasins and decided that they were numb.

He pulled the mitten on hurriedly and stood up. He was a bit frightened. He stamped up and down until the stinging returned into the feet. It certainly was cold, was his thought. That man from Sulphur Creek had spoken the truth when telling how cold it sometimes got in the country. And he had laughed at him at the time! That showed one must not be too sure of things. There was no mistake about it, it *was* cold. He strode up and down, stamping his feet and threshing his arms, until reassured by the returning warmth. Then he got out matches and proceeded to make a fire. From the undergrowth, where high water of the previous spring had lodged a supply of seasoned twigs, he got his fire-wood. Working carefully from a small beginning, he soon had a roaring fire, over which he thawed the ice from his face and in the protection of which he ate his biscuits. For the moment the cold of space was outwitted. The dog took satisfaction in the fire, stretching out close enough for warmth and far enough away to escape being singed.

When the man had finished, he filled his pipe and took his comfortable time over a smoke. Then he pulled on his mittens, settled the earflaps of his cap firmly about his ears, and took the creek trail up the left fork. The dog was disappointed and yearned back toward the fire. This man did not know cold. Possibly all the generations of his ancestry had been ignorant of cold, of real cold, of cold one hundred and seven degrees below freezing point. But the dog knew; all its ancestry knew, and it had inherited the knowledge. And it knew that it was not good to walk abroad in such fearful cold. It was the time to lie snug in a hole in the snow and wait for a curtain of cloud to be drawn across the face of outer space whence this cold came. On the other hand, there was no keen intimacy between the dog and the man. The one was the toil-slave of the other, and the only caresses it had ever received were the caresses of the whiplash and of harsh and menacing throat-sounds that threatened the whiplash. So the dog made no effort to communicate its apprehension to the man. It was not concerned in the welfare of the man; it was for its own sake that it yearned back toward the fire. But the man whistled, and spoke to it with the sound of whiplashes, and the dog swung in at the man's heels and followed after.

The man took a chew of tobacco and proceeded to start a new amber beard. Also, his moist breath quickly powdered with white his mustache, eyebrows, and lashes. There did not seem to be so many springs on the left fork of the Henderson, and for half an hour the man saw no signs of any. And then it happened. At a place where there were no signs, where the soft, unbroken snow seemed to advertise solidity beneath, the man broke through. It was not deep. He wet himself halfway to the knees before he floundered out to the firm crust.

He was angry, and cursed his luck aloud. He had hoped to get into camp with the boys at six o'clock, and this would delay him an hour, for he would have to build a fire and dry out his foot-gear. This was imperative at that low temperature—he knew that much; and he turned aside to the bank, which he climbed. On top, tangled in the underbrush about the trunks of several small spruce trees, was a high-water deposit of dry fire-wood—sticks and twigs, principally, but also larger portions of seasoned branches and fine, dry, last-year's grasses. He threw down several large pieces on top of the snow. This served for a foundation and prevented the young flame from drowning itself in the snow it otherwise would melt. The flame he got by touching a match to a small shred of birchbark that he took from his pocket. This burned even more readily than paper. Placing it on the foundation, he fed the young flame with wisps of dry grass and with the tiniest dry twigs.

He worked slowly and carefully, keenly aware of his danger. Gradually, as the flame grew stronger, he increased the size of the twigs with which he fed it. He squatted in the snow, pulling the twigs out from their entanglement in the brush and feeding directly to the flame. He knew there must be no failure. When it is seventy-five below zero, a man must not fail in his first attempt to build a fire—that is, if his feet are wet. If his feet are dry, and he fails, he can run along the trail for half a mile and restore his circulation. But the circulation of wet and freezing feet cannot be restored by running when it is seventy-five below. No matter how fast he runs, the wet feet will freeze the harder.

All this the man knew. The old timer on Sulphur Creek had told him about it the previous fall, and now he was appreciating the advice. Already all sensation had gone out of his feet. To build the fire he had been forced to remove his mittens, and the fingers had quickly gone numb. His pace of four miles an hour had kept his heart pumping blood to the surface of his body and to all the extremities. But the instant he

74

stopped, the action of the pump eased down. The cold of space smote the unprotected tip of the planet, and he, being on that unprotected tip, received the full force of the blow. The blood of his body recoiled before it. The blood was alive, like the dog, and like the dog it wanted to hide away and cover itself up from the fearful cold. So long as he walked four miles an hour, he pumped that blood, willy-nilly, to the surface; but now it ebbed away and sank down into the recesses of his body. The extremities were the first to feel its absence. His wet feet froze the faster, and his exposed fingers numbed the faster, though they had not yet begun to freeze. Nose and cheeks were already freezing, while the skin of all his body chilled as it lost its blood.

But he was safe. Toes and nose and cheeks would be only touched by the frost, for the fire was beginning to burn with strength. He was feeding it with twigs the size of his finger. In another minute he would be able to feed it with branches the size of his wrist, and then he could remove his wet foot-gear, and, while it dried, he could keep his naked feet warm by the fire, rubbing them at first, of course, with snow. The fire was a success. He was safe. He remembered the advice of the old-timer on Sulphur Creek, and smiled. The old-timer had been very serious in laying down the law that no man must travel alone in the Klondike after fifty below. Well, here he was; he had had the accident; he was alone; and he had saved himself. Those old-timers were rather womanish, some of them, he thought. All a man had to do was to keep his head, and he was all right. Any man who was a man could travel alone. But it was surprising, the rapidity with which his cheeks and nose were freezing. And he had not thought his fingers could go lifeless in so short a time. Lifeless they were, for he could scarcely make them move together to grip a twig, and they seemed remote from his body and from him. When he touched a twig, he had to look and see whether or not he had hold of it. The wires were pretty well down between him and his finger-ends.

All of which counted for little. There was the fire, snapping and crackling and promising life with every dancing flame. He started to untie his moccasins. They were coated with ice; the thick German socks were like sheaths of iron halfway to the knees; and the moccasin strings were like rods of steel all twisted and knotted as by some conflagration. For a moment he tugged with his numb fingers, then, realizing the folly of it, he drew his sheath-knife.

But before he could cut the strings, it happened. It was his own fault or, rather, his mistake. He should not have built the fire under the spruce tree. He should have built it in the open. But it had been easier to pull the twigs from the brush and drop them directly on the fire. Now the tree under which he had done this carried a weight of snow on its boughs. No wind had blown for weeks, and each bough was fully freighted. Each time he had pulled a twig he had communicated a slight agitation to the tree—an imperceptible agitation, so far as he was concerned, but an agitation sufficient to bring about the disaster. High up in the tree one bough capsized its load of snow. This fell on the boughs beneath, capsizing them. This process continued, spreading out and involving the whole tree. It grew like an avalanche, and it descended without warning upon the man and the fire, and the fire was blotted out! Where it had burned was a mantle of fresh and disordered snow.

The man was shocked. It was as though he had just heard his own sentence of death. For a moment he sat and stared at the spot where the fire had been. Then he grew very calm. Perhaps the old-timer on Sulphur Creek was right. If he had only had a trail-mate he would have been in no danger now. The trail-mate could have built the fire. Well, it was up to him to build the fire over again, and this second time there must be no failure. Even if he succeeded, he would most likely lose some toes. His feet must be badly frozen by now, and there would be some time before the second fire was ready.

Such were his thoughts, but he did not sit and think them. He was busy all the time they were passing through his mind. He made a new foundation for a fire, this time in the open, where no treacherous tree could blot it out. Next, he gathered dry grasses and tiny twigs from the high-water flotsam. He could not bring his fingers together to pull them out, but he was able to gather them by the handful. In this way he got many rotten twigs and bits of green moss that were undesirable, but it was the best he could do. He worked methodically, even collecting an armful of the larger branches to be used later when the fire gathered strength. And all the while the dog sat and watched him, a certain yearning wistfulness in its eyes, for it looked upon him as the fire-provider, and the fire was slow in coming.

When all was ready, the man reached in his pocket for a second piece of birch-bark. He knew the bark was there, and, though he could not feel it with his fingers, he could hear its crisp rustling as he fumbled for it. Try as he would, he could not clutch hold of it. And all the time, in his consciousness, was the knowledge that each instant his feet were freezing. This thought tended to put him in a panic, but he fought against it and kept calm. He pulled on his mittens with his teeth, and threshed his arms back and forth, beating his hands with all his might against his sides. He did this sitting down, and he stood up to do it; and all the while the dog sat in the snow, its wolf-brush of a tail curled around warmly over its forefeet, its sharp wolf-ears pricked forward intently as it watched the man. And the man as he beat and threshed with his arms and hands, felt a great surge of envy as he regarded the creature that was warm and secure in its natural covering.

After a time he was aware of the first far-away signals of sensation in his beaten fingers. The faint tingling grew stronger till it evolved into a stinging ache that was excruciating, but which the man hailed with satisfaction. He stripped the mitten from his right hand and fetched forth the birch-bark. The exposed fingers were quickly going numb again. Next he brought out his bunch of sulphur matches. But the tremendous cold had already driven the life out of his fingers. In his effort to separate one match from the others, the whole bunch fell in the snow. He tried to pick it out of the snow, but failed. The dead fingers could neither touch nor clutch. He was very careful. He drove the thought of his freezing feet, and nose, and cheeks, out of his mind, devoting his whole soul to the matches. He watched, using the sense of vision in place of that of touch, and when he saw his fingers on each side the bunch, he closed them—that is, he willed to close them, for the wires were down, and the fingers did not obey. He pulled the mitten on the right hand, and beat it fiercely against his knee. Then, with both mittened hands, he scooped the bunch of matches, along with much snow, into his lap. Yet he was no better off.

After some manipulation he managed to get the bunch between the heels of his mittened hands. In this fashion he carried it to his mouth. The ice crackled and snapped when by a violent effort he opened his mouth. He drew the lower jaw in, curled the upper lip out of the way, and scraped the bunch with his upper teeth in order to separate a match. He succeeded in getting one, which he dropped on his lap. He was no better off. He could not pick it up. Then he devised a way. He picked it up in his teeth and scratched it on his leg. Twenty times he scratched before he succeeded in lighting it. As it flamed he held it with his teeth to the birch-bark. But the burning brimstone went up his nostrils and into his lungs, causing him to cough spasmodically. The match fell into the snow and went out.

The old-timer on Sulphur Creek was right, he thought in the moment of controlled despair that ensued; after fifty below, a man should travel with a partner. He beat his hands, but failed in exciting any sensation. Suddenly he bared both his hands, removing the mittens with his teeth. He caught the whole bunch between the heels of his hands. His arm-muscles not being frozen enabled him to press the hand-heels tightly against the matches. Then he scratched the bunch along his leg. It flared into flame, seventy sulphur matches at once! There was no wind to blow them out. He kept his head to one side to escape the strangling fumes, and held the blazing bunch to the birch-bark. As he so held it, he became aware of sensation in his hand. His flesh was burning. He could smell it. Deep down below the surface he could feel it. The sensation developed into pain that grew acute. And still he endured it, holding the flame of the matches clumsily to the bark that would not light readily because his own burning hands were in the way, absorbing most of the flame.

At last, when he could endure no more, he jerked his hands apart. The blazing matches fell sizzling into the snow, but the birch-bark was alight. He began laying dry grasses and the tiniest twigs on the flame. He could not pick and choose, for he had to lift the fuel between the heels of his hands. Small pieces of rotten wood and green moss clung to the twigs, and he bit them off as well as he could with his teeth. He cherished the flame carefully and awkwardly. It meant life, and it must not perish. The withdrawal of blood from the surface of his body now made him begin to shiver, and he grew more awkward. A large piece of green moss fell squarely on the little fire. He tried to poke it out with his fingers, but his shivering frame made him poke too far, and he disrupted the nucleus of the little fire, the burning grasses and tiny twigs separating and scattering. He tried to poke them together again, but in spite of the tenseness of the effort, his shivering got away with him, and the twigs were hopelessly scattered. Each twig gushed a puff of smoke and went out. The fire-provider had failed. As he looked apathetically about him, his eyes chanced on the dog, sitting across the ruins of the fire from him, in the snow, making restless, hunching movement, slightly lifting one forefoot and then the other, shifting its weight back and forth on them with wistful eagerness.

The sight of the dog put a wild idea into his head.

He remembered the tale of the man, caught in a blizzard, who killed a steer and crawled inside the carcass, and so was saved. He would kill the dog and bury his hands in the warm body until the numbness went out of them. Then he could build another fire. He spoke to the dog, calling it to him; but in his voice was a strange note of fear that frightened the animal, who had never known the man to speak in such way before. Something was the matter, and its suspicious nature sensed danger—it knew not what danger, but somewhere, somehow, in its brain arose an apprehension of the man. It flattened its ears down at the sound of the man's voice, and its restless, hunching movements and the liftings and shiftings of its forefeet became more pronounced; but it would not come to the man. He got on his hands and knees and crawled toward the dog. This unusual posture again excited suspicion, and the animal sidled mincingly away.

The man sat up in the snow for a moment and struggled for calmness. Then he pulled on his mittens, by means of his teeth, and got upon his feet. He glanced down at first in order to assure himself that he was really standing up, for the absence of sensation in his feet left him unrelated to the earth. His erect position in itself started to drive the webs of suspicion from the dog's mind; and when he spoke peremptorily, with the sound of whiplashes in his voice, the dog rendered its customary allegiance and came to him. As it came within reaching distance, the man lost his control. His arms flashed out to the dog, and he experienced genuine surprise when he discovered that his hands could not clutch, that there was neither bend nor feeling in the fingers. He had forgotten for the moment that they were frozen and that they were freezing more and more. All this happened quickly, and before the animal could get away, he encircled its body with his arms. He sat down in the snow, and in this fashion held the dog, while it snarled and whined and struggled.

But it was all he could do, hold its body encircled in his arms and sit there. He realized that he could not kill the dog. There was no way to do it. With his helpless hands he could neither draw nor hold his sheathknife nor throttle the animal. He released it, it plunged wildly away, with tail between its legs, and still snarling. It halted forty feet away and surveyed him curiously, with ears sharply pricked forward. The man looked down at his hands in order to locate them, and found them hanging on the ends of his arms. It struck him as curious that one should have to use his eyes in order to find out where his hands were. He began threshing his arms back and forth, beating the mittened hands against his sides. He did this for five minutes, violently, and his heart pumped enough blood up to the surface to put a stop to his shivering. But no sensation was aroused in the hands. He had an impression that they hung like weights on the ends of his arms, but when he tried to run the impression down, he could not find it.

A certain fear of death, dull and oppressive, came to him. This fear quickly became poignant as he realized that it was no longer a mere matter of freezing his fingers and toes, or of losing his hands and feet, but that it was a matter of life and death with the chances against him. This threw him into a panic, and he turned and ran up the creek-bed along the old dim trail. The dog joined in behind and kept up with him. He ran blindly, without intention, in fear such as he had never known in his life. Slowly, as he ploughed and floundered through the snow, he began to see things again, —the banks of the creek, the old timber-jams, the leafless aspens, and the sky. The running made him feel better. He did not shiver. Maybe, if he ran on, his feet would thaw out; and, anyway, if he ran far enough, he would reach camp and the boys. Without doubt he would lose some fingers and toes and some of his face; but the boys would take care of him, and save the rest of him when he got there. And at the same time there was another thought in his mind that said he would never get to the camp and the boys; that it was too many miles away, that the freezing had too great a start on him, and that he would soon be stiff and dead. This thought he kept in the background and refused to consider. Sometimes it pushed itself forward and demanded to be heard, but he thrust it back and strove to think of other things.

It struck him as curious that he could run at all on feet so frozen that he could not feel them when they struck the earth and took the weight of his body. He seemed to himself to skim along above the surface, and to have no connection with the earth. Somewhere he had once seen a winged Mercury, and he wondered if Mercury felt as he felt when skimming over the earth.

His theory of running until he reached camp and the boys had one flaw in it: he lacked the endurance. Several times he stumbled, and finally he tottered, crumpled up, and fell. When he tried to rise, he failed. He must sit and rest, he decided, and next time he would merely walk and keep on going. As he sat and regained his breath, he noted that he was feeling quite warm and comfortable. He was not shivering, and it even seemed that a warm glow had come to his chest and trunk. And yet, when he touched his nose or cheeks, there was no sensation. Running would not thaw them out. Nor would it thaw out his hands and feet. Then the thought came to him that the frozen portions of his body must be extending. He tried to keep this thought down, to forget it, to think of something else; he was aware of the panicky feeling that it caused, and he was afraid of the panic. But the thought asserted itself, and persisted, until it produced a vision of his body totally frozen. This was too much, and he made another wild run along the trail. Once he slowed down to a walk, but the thought of the freezing extending itself made him run again.

And all the time the dog ran with him, at his heels. When he fell down a second time, it curled its tail over its forefeet and sat in front of him, facing him, curiously eager and intent. The warmth and security of the animal angered him, and he cursed it till it flattened down its ears appeasingly. This time the shivering came more quickly upon the man. He was losing in his battle with the frost. It was creeping into his body from all sides. The thought of it drove him on, but he ran no more than a hundred feet, when he staggered and pitched headlong. It was his last panic. When he had recovered his breath and control, he sat up and entertained in his mind the conception of meeting death with dignity. However, the conception did not come to him in such terms. His idea of it was that he had been making a fool of himself, running around like a chicken with its head cut off—such was the simile that occurred to him. Well he was bound to freeze anyway, and he might as well take it decently. With this new-found peace of mind came the first glimmerings of drowsiness. A good idea, he thought, to sleep off to death. It was like taking an anaesthetic. Freezing was not so bad as people thought. There were lots worse ways to die.

He pictured the boys finding his body next day. Suddenly he found himself with them, coming along the trail and looking for himself. And, still with them, he came around a turn in the trail and found himself lying in the snow. He did not belong with himself any more, for even then he was out of himself, standing with the boys and looking at himself in the snow. It certainly was cold, was his thought. When he got back to the States he could tell the folks what real cold was. He drifted on from this to a vision of the old-timer on Sulphur Creek. He could see him quite clearly, warm and comfortable, and smoking a pipe.

"You were right, old hoss; you were right," the man mumbled to the old-timer of Sulphur Creek.

Then the man drowsed off into what seemed to him the most comfortable and satisfying sleep he had ever known. The dog sat facing him and waiting. The brief day drew to a close in a long, slow twilight. There were no signs of a fire to be made, and, besides, never in the dog's experience had it known a man to sit like that in the snow and make no fire. As the twilight drew on, its eager yearning for the fire mastered it, and with a great lifting and shifting of forefeet, it whined softly, then flattened its ears down in anticipation of being chided by the man. But the man remained silent. Later, the dog whined loudly. And still later it crept close to the man and caught the scent of death. This made the animal bristle and back away. A little longer it delayed, howling under the stars that leaped and danced and shone brightly in the cold sky. Then it turned and trotted up the trail in the direction of the camp it knew, where were the other food-providers and fire-providers.

The Body-Snatcher

As he did so his eyes lighted on the dead face. He started; he took two steps nearer, with the candle raised.

Every night in the year, four of us sat in the small parlour of the George at Debenham—the undertaker, and the landlord, and Fettes, and myself. Sometimes there would be more; but blow high, blow low, come rain or snow or frost, we four would be each planted in his own particular armchair. Fettes was an old drunken Scotchman, a man of education obviously, and a man of some property, since he lived in idleness. He had come to Debenham years ago, while still young, and by a mere continuance of living had grown to be an adopted townsman. His blue camlet cloak was a local antiquity, like the church-spire. His place in the parlour at the George, his absence from church, his old, crapulous, disreputable vices, were all things of course in Debenham. He had some vague Radical opinions and some fleeting infidelities, which he would now and again set forth and emphasise with tottering slaps upon the table. He drank rum—five glasses regularly every evening; and for the greater portion of his nightly visit to the George sat, with his glass in his right hand, in a state of melancholy alcoholic saturation. We called him the Doctor, for he was supposed to have some special knowledge of medicine, and had been known, upon a pinch, to set a fracture or reduce a dislocation; but beyond these slight particulars, we had no knowledge of his character and antecedents.

One dark winter night—it had struck nine some time before the landlord joined us—there was a sick man in the George, a great neighbouring proprietor suddenly struck down with apoplexy on his way to Parliament; and the great man's still greater London doctor had been telegraphed to his bedside. It was the first time that such a thing had happened in Debenham, for the railway was but newly open, and we were all proportionately moved by the occurrence.

"He's come," said the landlord, after he had filled and lighted his pipe.

"He?" said I. "Who?—not the doctor?"

"Himself," replied our host.

"What is his name?"

"Doctor Macfarlane," said the landlord.

Fettes was far through his third tumbler, stupidly fuddled, now nodding over, now staring mazily around him; but at the last word he seemed to awaken, and repeated the name "Macfarlane" twice, quietly enough the first time, but with sudden emotion at the second.

"Yes," said the landlord, "that's his name, Doctor Wolfe Macfarlane."

88

Fettes became instantly sober; his eyes awoke, his voice became clear, loud, and steady, his language forcible and earnest. We were all startled by the transformation, as if a man had arisen from the dead.

"I beg your pardon," he said, "I am afraid I have not been paying much attention to your talk. Who is this Wolfe Macfarlane?" And then, when he had heard the landlord out, "It cannot be, it cannot be," he added; "and yet I would like well to see him face to face."

"Do you know him, Doctor?" asked the undertaker, with a gasp.

"God forbid!" was the reply. "And yet the name is a strange one; it were too much to fancy two. Tell me, landlord, is he old?"

"Well," said the host, "he's not a young man, to be sure, and his hair is white; but he looks younger than you."

"He is older, though; years older. But," with a slap upon the table, "it's the rum you see in my face—rum and sin. This man, perhaps, may have an easy conscience and a good digestion. Conscience! Hear me speak. You would think I was some good, old, decent Christian, would you not? But no, not I; I never canted. Voltaire might have canted if he'd stood in my shoes; but the brains"—with a rattling fillip on his bald head—"the brains were clear and active, and I saw and made no deductions."

"If you know this doctor," I ventured to remark, after a somewhat awful pause, "I should gather that you do not share the landlord's good opinion."

Fettes paid no regard to me.

"Yes," he said, with sudden decision, "I must see him face to face."

There was another pause, and then a door was closed rather sharply on the first floor, and a step was heard upon the stair.

"That's the doctor," cried the landlord. "Look sharp, and you can catch him."

It was but two steps from the small parlour to the door of the old George Inn; the wide oak staircase landed almost in the street; there was room for a Turkey rug and nothing more between the threshold and the last round of the descent; but this little space was every evening brilliantly lit up, not only by the light upon the stair and the great signal-lamp below the sign, but by the warm radiance of the bar-room window. The George thus brightly advertised itself to passers-by in the cold street. Fettes walked steadily to the spot, and we, who were hanging behind, beheld the two men meet, as one of them had phrased it, face to face. Dr. Macfarlane was alert and vigorous. His white hair set off his pale and placid, although energetic, countenance. He was richly dressed in the finest of broadcloth and the whitest of linen, with a great gold watch-chain and studs and spectacles of the same precious material. He wore a broad-folded tie, white and speckled with lilac, and he carried on his arm a comfortable driving-coat of fur. There was no doubt but he became his years, breathing, as he did, of wealth and consideration; and it was a surprising contrast to see our parlour sot—bald, dirty, pimpled, and robed in his old camlet cloak—confront him at the bottom of the stairs.

"Macfarlane!" he said somewhat loudly, more like a herald than a friend.

The great doctor pulled up short on the fourth step,

as though the familiarity of the address surprised and somewhat shocked his dignity.

"Toddy Macfarlane!" repeated Fettes.

The London man almost staggered. He stared for the swiftest of seconds at the man before him, glanced behind him with a sort of scare, and then in a startled whisper, "Fettes!" he said, "you!"

"Ay," said the other, "me! Did you think I was dead too? We are not so easy shut of our acquaintance."

"Hush, hush!" exclaimed the doctor. "Hush, hush! this meeting is so unexpected—I can see you are unmanned. I hardly knew you, I confess, at first; but I am overjoyed—overjoyed to have this opportunity. For the present it must be how-d'ye-do and good-bye in one, for my fly is waiting, and I must not fail the train; but you shall—let me see—yes—you shall give me your address, and you can count on early news of me. We must do something for you, Fettes. I fear you are out at elbows; but we must see to that for auld lang syne, as once we sang at suppers."

"Money!" cried Fettes; "money from you! The money that I had from you is lying where I cast it in the rain."

Dr. Macfarlane had talked himself into some measure of superiority and confidence, but the uncommon energy of this refusal cast him back into his first confusion.

A horrible, ugly look came and went across his almost venerable countenance. "My dear fellow," he said, "be it as you please; my last thought is to offend you. I would intrude on none. I will leave you my address, however—"

"I do not wish it—I do not wish to know the roof that shelters you," interrupted the other. "I heard your name; I feared it might be you, I wished to know if, after all, there were a God; I know now that there is none. Begone!"

He still stood in the middle of the rug, between the stair and doorway; and the great London physician, in order to escape, would be forced to step to one side. It was plain that he hesitated before the thought of this humiliation. White as he was, there was a dangerous glitter in his spectacles; but while he still paused uncertain, he became aware that the driver of his fly was peering in from the street at this unusual scene and caught a glimpse at the same time of our little body from the parlour, huddled by the corner of the bar. The presence of so many witnesses decided him at once to flee. He crouched together, brushing on the wainscot, and made a dart like a serpent, striking for the door. But his tribulation was not yet entirely at an end, for even as he was passing Fettes clutched him by the arm and these words came in a whisper, and yet painfully distinct, "Have you seen it again?"

The great rich London doctor cried out aloud with a sharp, throttling cry; he dashed his questioner across the open space, and, with his hands over his head, fled out of the door like a detected thief. Before it had occurred to one of us to make a movement the fly was already rattling toward the station. The scene was over like a dream, but the dream had left proofs and traces of its passage. Next day the servant found the fine gold spectacles broken on the threshold, and that very night we were all standing breathless by the bar-room window, and Fettes at our side, sober, pale, and resolute in look.

"God protect us, Mr. Fettes!" said the landlord, coming first into possession of his customary senses. "What in the universe is all this? These are strange things you have been saying."

Fettes turned toward us; he looked us each in succession in the face. "See if you can hold your tongues," said he. "That man Macfarlane is not safe to cross; those that have done so already have repented it too late."

And then, without so much as finishing his third glass, far less waiting for the other two, he bade us good-bye and went forth, under the lamp of the hotel, into the black night.

We three turned to our places in the parlour, with the big red fire and four clear candles; and as we recapitulated what had passed, the first chill of our surprise soon changed into a glow of curiosity. We sat late; it was the latest session I have known in the old George. Each man, before we parted, had his theory that he was bound to prove; and none of us had any nearer business in this world than to track out the past of our condemned companion, and surprise the secret that he shared with the great London doctor. It is no great boast, but I believe I was a better hand at worming out a story than either of my fellows at the George; and perhaps there is now no other man alive who could narrate to you the following foul and unnatural events.

In his young days Fettes studied medicine in the schools of Edinburgh. He had talent of a kind, the talent that picks up swiftly what it hears and readily retails it for its own. He worked little at home; but he was civil, attentive, and intelligent in the presence of his masters. They soon picked him out as a lad who listened closely and remembered well; nay, strange as it seemed to me when I first heard it, he was in those days well favoured, and pleased by his exterior. There was, at that period, a certain extra-mural teacher of anatomy, whom I shall here designate by the letter K. His name was subsequently too well known. The man who bore it skulked through the streets of Edinburgh in disguise, while the mob that applauded at the execution of Burke called loudly for the blood of his employer. But Mr. K—— was then at the top of his vogue; he enjoyed a popularity due partly to his own talent and address, partly to the incapacity of his rival, the university professor. The students, at least, swore by his name, and Fettes believed himself, and was believed by others, to have laid the foundations of success when he had acquired the favour of this meteorically famous man. Mr. K—— was a *bon vivant* as well as an accomplished teacher; he liked a sly illusion no less than a careful preparation. In both capacities Fettes enjoyed and deserved his notice, and by the second year of his attendance he held the half-regular position of second demonstrator or sub-assistant in his class.

In this capacity the charge of the theatre and lecture-room devolved in particular upon his shoulders. He had to answer for the cleanliness of the premises and the conduct of the other students, and it was a part of his duty to supply, receive, and divide the various subjects. It was with a view to this last—at that time very delicate—affair that he was lodged by Mr. K—— in the same wynd, and at last in the same building, with the dissecting-rooms. Here, after a night of turbulent pleasures, his hand still tottering, his sight still misty and confused, he would be called out of bed in the black hours before the winter dawn by the unclean and desperate interlopers who supplied the table. He would open the door to these men, since infamous throughout the land. He would help them with their tragic burden, pay them their sordid price, and remain alone, when they were gone, with the unfriendly relics of humanity. From such a scene he would return to snatch another hour or two of slumber, to repair the abuses of the night, and refresh himself for the labours of the day.

Few lads could have been more insensible to the impressions of a life thus passed among the ensigns of mortality. His mind was closed against all general considerations. He was incapable of interest in the fate and fortunes of another, the slave of his own desires and low ambitions. Cold, light, and selfish in the last resort, he had that modicum of prudence, miscalled morality, which keeps a man from inconvenient drunkenness or punishable theft. He coveted, besides, a measure of consideration from his masters and his fellow-pupils, and he had no desire to fail conspicuously in the external parts of life. Thus he made it his pleasure to gain some distinction in his studies, and day after day rendered unimpeachable eye-service to his employer, Mr. K——. For his day of work he indemnified himself by nights of roaring, blackguardly enjoyment; and when that balance had been struck, the organ that he called his conscience declared itself content.

The supply of subjects was a continual trouble to him as well as to his master. In that large and busy class, the raw material of the anatomists kept perpetually running out; and the business thus rendered necessary was not only unpleasant in itself, but threatened dangerous consequences to all who were concerned. It was the policy of Mr. K—— to ask no questions in his dealings with the trade. "They bring the body, and we pay the price," he used to say, dwelling on the alliteration—"*quid pro quo.*" And, again, and somewhat profanely, "Ask no questions," he would tell his assistants, "for conscience' sake." There was no understanding that the subjects were provided by the crime of murder. Had that idea been broached to him in words, he would have recoiled in horror; but the lightness of his speech upon so grave a matter was, in itself, an offence against good manners, and a temptation to the men with whom he dealt. Fettes, for instance, had often remarked to himself upon the singular freshness of the bodies. He had been struck again and again by the hang-dog, abominable looks of the ruffians who came to him before the dawn; and putting things together clearly in his private thoughts, he perhaps attributed a meaning too immoral and too categorical to the unguarded counsels of his master. He understood his duty, in short, to have three branches: to take what was brought, to pay the price, and to avert the eye from any evidence of crime.

One November morning this policy of silence was put sharply to the test. He had been awake all night with a racking toothache—pacing his room like a caged beast or throwing himself in fury on his bed—and had fallen at last into that profound, uneasy slumber that so often follows on a night of pain, when he was awakened by the third or fourth angry repetition of the concerted signal. There was a thin, bright moonshine; it was bitter cold, windy, and frosty; the town had not yet awakened, but an indefinable stir already preluded the noise and business of the day. The ghouls had come later than usual, and they seemed more than usually eager to be gone. Fettes, sick with sleep, lighted them upstairs. He heard their grumbling Irish voices through a dream; and as they stripped the sack from their sad merchandise he leaned dozing, with his shoulder propped against the wall; he had to shake himself to find the men their money. As he did so his eyes lighted on the dead face. He started; he took two steps nearer, with the candle raised.

"God Almighty!" he cried. "That is Jane Galbraith!"

The men answered nothing, but they shuffled nearer the door.

"I know her, I tell you," he continued. "She was alive and hearty yesterday. It's impossible she can be dead; it's impossible you should have got this body fairly."

"Sure, sir, you're mistaken entirely," said one of the men.

But the other looked Fettes darkly in the eyes, and demanded the money on the spot.

It was impossible to misconceive the threat or to exaggerate the danger. The lad's heart failed him. He stammered some excuses. Counted out the sum, and saw his hateful visitors depart. No sooner were they gone than he hastened to confirm his doubts. By a dozen unquestionable marks he identified the girl he had jested with the day before. He saw, with horror, marks upon her body that might well betoken violence. A panic seized him, and he took refuge in his room. There he reflected at length over the discovery that he had made: considered soberly the bearing of Mr. K——'s instructions and the danger to himself of interference in so serious a business, and at last, in sore perplexity, determined to wait for the advice of his immediate superior, the class assistant.

This was a young doctor, Wolfe Macfarlane, a high favourite among all the reckless students, clever, dissipated, and unscrupulous to the last degree. He had travelled and studied abroad. His manners were agreeable and a little forward. He was an authority on the stage, skillful on the ice or the links with skate or golf-club; he dressed with nice audacity, and, to put the finishing touch upon his glory, he kept a gig and a strong trotting-horse. With Fettes he was on terms of intimacy; indeed, their relative positions called for some community of life; and when subjects were scarce the pair would drive far into the country in Macfarlane's gig, visit and desecrate some lonely graveyard, and return before dawn with their booty to the door of the dissecting-room.

On that particular morning Macfarlane arrived somewhat earlier than his wont. Fettes heard him, and met him on the stairs, told him his story, and showed him the cause of his alarm. Macfarlane examined the marks on her body.

"Yes," he said with a nod, "it looks fishy."

"Well, what should I do?" asked Fettes.

"Do?" repeated the other. "Do you want to do anything? Least said soonest mended, I should say."

"Someone else might recognise her," objected Fettes. "She was as well known as the Castle Rock."

"We'll hope not," said Macfarlane, "and if anybody does—well, you didn't, don't you see, and there's an end. The fact is, this has been going on too long. Stir up the mud, and you'll get K—— into the most unholy trouble; you'll be in a shocking box yourself. So will I, if you come to that. I should like to know how any one of us would look, or what the devil we should have to say for ourselves, in any Christian witness-box. For me, you know, there's one thing certain—that, practically speaking, all our subjects have been murdered."

"Macfarlane!" cried Fettes.

"Come now!" sneered the other. "As if you hadn't suspected it yourself!"

"Suspecting is one thing—"

"And proof another. Yes, I know; and I'm as sorry as you are this should have come here," tapping the body with his cane. "The next best thing for me is not to recognise it; and," he added coolly, "I don't. You may, if you please. I don't dictate, but I think a man of the world would do as I do; and I may add, I fancy that is what K—— would look for at our hands. The question is, Why did he choose us two for his assistants? And I answer, because he didn't want old wives."

This was the tone of all others to affect the mind of a lad like Fettes. He agreed to imitate Macfarlane. The body of the unfortunate girl was duly dissected, and no one remarked or appeared to recognise her.

One afternoon, when his day's work was over, Fettes dropped into a popular tavern and found Macfarlane sitting with a stranger. This was a small man, very pale and dark, with coal-black eyes. The cut of his features gave a promise of intellect and refinement which was but feebly realised in his manners, for he proved, upon a nearer acquaintance, coarse, vulgar, and stupid. He exercised, however, a very remarkable control over Macfarlane; issued orders like the Great Bashaw; became inflamed at the least discussion or delay, and commented rudely on the servility with which he was obeyed. This most offensive person took a fancy to Fettes on the spot, plied him with drinks, and honoured him with unusual confidences on his past career. If a tenth part of what he confessed were true, he was a very loathsome rogue; and the lad's vanity was tickled by the attention of so experienced a man.

"I'm a pretty bad fellow myself," the stranger remarked, "but Macfarlane is the boy—Toddy Macfarlane I call him. Toddy, order your friend another glass." Or it might be, "Toddy, you jump up and shut the door." "Toddy hates me," he said again. "Oh, yes, Toddy, you do!"

"Don't you call me that confounded name," growled Macfarlane.

"Hear him! Did you ever see the lads play knife? He would like to do that all over my body," remarked the stranger.

"We medicals have a better way than that," said Fettes. "When we dislike a dead friend of ours, we dissect him."

Macfarlane looked up sharply, as though this jest were scarcely to his mind.

The afternoon passed. Gray, for that was the stranger's name, invited Fettes to join them at dinner, ordered a feast so sumptuous that the tavern was thrown into commotion, and when all was done commanded Macfarlane to settle the bill. It was late before they separated; the man Gray was incapably drunk. Macfarlane, sobered by his fury, chewed the cud of the money he had been forced to squander and the slights he had been obliged to swallow. Fettes, with various liquors singing in his head, returned home with devious footsteps and a mind entirely in abeyance.

Next day Macfarlane was absent from the class, and Fettes smiled to himself as he imagined him still squiring the intolerable Gray from tavern to tavern. As soon as the hour of liberty had struck, he posted from place to place in quest of his last night's companions. He could find them, however, nowhere; so returned early to his rooms, went early to bed, and slept the sleep of the just.

At four in the morning he was awakened by the well-known signal. Descending to the door, he was filled with astonishment to find Macfarlane with his gig, and in the gig one of those long and ghastly packages with which he was so well aquainted.

"What?" he cried. "Have you been out alone? How did you manage?"

But Macfarlane silenced him roughly, bidding him turn to business. When they had got the body upstairs and laid it on the table, Macfarlane made at first as if he were going away. Then he paused and seemed to hesitate; and then, "You had better look at the face," said he, in tones of some constraint. "You had better," he repeated, as Fettes only stared at him in wonder.

"But where, and how, and when did you come by it?" cried the other.

"Look at the face," was the only answer.

Fettes was staggered; strange doubts assailed him. He looked from the young doctor to the body, and then back again. At last, with a start, he did as he was bidden. He had almost expected the sight that met his eyes, and yet the shock was cruel. To see, fixed in the rigidity of death and naked on that coarse layer of sackcloth, the man whom he had left well clad and full of meat and sin upon the threshold of a tavern, awoke, even in the thoughtless Fettes, some of the terrors of the conscience. It was a *cras tibi* which re-echoed in his soul, that two whom he had known should have come to lie upon these icy tables. Yet these were only secondary thoughts. His first concern regarded Wolfe. Unprepared for a challenge so momentous, he knew not how to look his comrade in the face. He durst not meet his eye, and he had neither words nor voice at his command.

It was Macfarlane himself who made the first advance. He came up quietly behind and laid his hand gently but firmly on the other's shoulder.

"Richardson," said he, "may have the head."

Now, Richardson was a student who had long been anxious for that portion of the human subject to dissect. There was no answer, and the murderer resumed: "Talking of business, you must pay me; your accounts, you see, must tally."

Fettes found a voice, the ghost of his own: "Pay you!" he cried. "Pay you for that?"

"Why, yes, of course you must. By all means and on every possible account, you must," returned the other. "I dare not give it for nothing, you dare not take it for nothing; it would compromise us both. This is another case like Jane Galbraith's. The more things are wrong, the more we must act as if all were right. Where does old K—— keep his money?"

"There," answered Fettes hoarsely, pointing to a cupboard in the corner.

"Give me the key, then," said the other calmly, holding out his hand.

There was an instant's hesitation, and the die was cast. Macfarlane could not suppress a nervous twitch, the infinitesimal mark of an immense relief, as he felt the key between his fingers. He opened the cupboard, brought out pen and ink and a paper-book that stood in one compartment, and separated from the funds in a drawer a sum suitable to the occasion.

"Now, look here," he said, "there is the payment made—first proof of your good faith; first step to your security. You have now to clinch it by a second. Enter the payment in your book, and then you for your part may defy the devil."

The next few seconds were for Fettes an agony of thought; but in balancing his terrors it was the most immediate that triumphed. Any future difficulty seemed almost welcome if he could avoid a present quarrel with Macfarlane. He set down the candle which he had been carrying all this time, and with a steady hand entered the date, the nature, and the amount of the transaction.

"And now," said Macfarlane, "it's only fair that you should pocket the lucre. I've had my share already. By-the-bye, when a man of the world falls into a bit of luck, has a few shillings extra in his pocket —I'm ashamed to speak of it, but there's a rule of conduct in the case. No treating, no purchase of expensive class-books, no squaring of old debts; borrow, don't lend."

"Macfarlane," began Fettes, still somewhat hoarsely, "I have put my neck in a halter to oblige you."

"To oblige me?" cried Wolfe. "Oh, come! You did, as near as I can see the matter, what you down-right had to do in self-defence. Suppose I got into trouble, where would you be? This second little matter flows clearly from the first. Mr. Gray is the continuation of Miss Galbraith. You can't begin and then stop. If you begin, you must keep on beginning; that's the truth. No rest for the wicked."

A horrible sense of blackness and the treachery of fate seized hold upon the soul of the unhappy student.

"My God!" he cried, "but what have I done? and when did I begin? To be made a class assistant—in the name of reason, where's the harm in that? Service wanted the position; Service might have got it. Would *he* have been where *I* am now?"

"My dear fellow," said Macfarlane, "what a boy you are! What harm *has* come to you? What harm *can* come to you if you hold your tongue? Why, man, do you know what this life is? There are two squads of us—the lions and the lambs. If you're a lamb, you'll come to lie upon these tables like Gray or Jane Galbraith; if you're a lion, you'll live and drive a horse like me, like K——, like all the world with any wit or courage. You're staggered at the first. But look at K——! My dear fellow, you're clever, you have pluck. I like you, and K—— likes you. You were born to lead the hunt; and I tell you, on my honour and my experience of life, three days from now you'll laugh at all these scarecrows like a High School boy at a farce."

And with that Macfarlane took his departure and drove off up the wynd in his gig to get under cover before daylight. Fettes was thus left alone with his regrets. He saw the miserable peril in which he stood involved. He saw, with inexpressible dismay, that there was no limit to his weakness, and that, from concession to concession, he had fallen from the arbiter

of Macfarlane's destiny to his paid and helpless accomplice. He would have given the world to have been
a little braver at the time, but it did not occur to him
that he might still be brave. The secret of Jane Galbraith and the cursed entry in the day-book closed his
mouth.

Hours passed; the class began to arrive; the members of the unhappy Gray were dealt out to one and
to another, and received without remark. Richardson
was made happy with the head; and before the hour of
freedom rang, Fettes trembled with exultation to perceive how far they had already gone toward safety.

For two days he continued to watch, with increasing
joy, the dreadful process of disguise.

On the third day Macfarlane made his appearance.
He had been ill, he said; but he made up for lost time
by the energy with which he directed the students. To
Richardson in particular he extended the most valuable
assistance and advice, and that student, encouraged by
the praise of the demonstrator, burned high with am-
bitious hopes, and saw the medal already in his grasp.

Before the week was out Macfarlane's prophecy
had been fulfilled. Fettes had outlived his terrors and
had forgotten his baseness. He began to plume himself
upon his courage, and had so arranged the story in
his mind that he could look back on these events with
an unhealthy pride. Of his accomplice he saw but little.
They met, of course, in the business of the class; they
received their orders together from Mr. K——. At
times they had a word or two in private, and Macfarlane was from first to last particularly kind and jovial.
But it was plain that he avoided any reference to their
common secret; and even when Fettes whispered to

him that he had cast in his lot with the lions and for-sworn the lambs, he only signed to him smilingly to hold his peace.

At length an occasion arose which threw the pair once more into a closer union. Mr. K—— was again short of subjects; pupils were eager, and it was a part of this teacher's pretensions to be always well sup-plied. At the same time there came the news of burial in the rustic graveyard of Glencorse. Time has little changed the place in question. It stood then, as now, upon a crossroad, out of call of human habitations, and buried fathom deep in the foliage of six cedar trees. The cries of the sheep upon the neighbouring hills, the streamlets upon either hand, one loudly singing among pebbles, the other dripping furtively from pond to pond, the stir of the wind in mountainous old flower-ing chestnuts, and once in seven days the voice of the bell and the old tunes of the precentor, were the only sounds that disturbed the silence around the rural church. The Resurrection Man—to use a byname of the period—was not to be deterred by any of the sanctities of customary piety. It was part of his trade to despise and desecrate the scrolls and trumpets of old tombs, the paths worn by the feet of worshippers and mourners, and the offerings and the inscriptions of bereaved affection. To rustic neighbourhoods, where love is more than commonly tenacious, and where some bonds of blood or fellowship unite the entire society of a parish, the body-snatcher, far from being repelled by natural respect, was attracted by the ease and safety of the task. To bodies that had been laid in earth, in joyful expectation of a far different awak-ening, there came that hasty, lamp-lit, terror-haunted resurrection of the spade and mattock. The coffin was forced, the cerements torn, and the melancholy relics, clad in sackcloth, after being rattled for hours on moonless byways, were at length exposed to uttermost indignities before a class of gaping boys.

Somewhat as two vultures may swoop upon a dying lamb, Fettes and Macfarlane were to be let loose upon a grave in that green and quiet resting-place. The wife of a farmer, a woman who had lived for sixty years, and been known for nothing but good butter and a godly conversation, was to be rooted from her grave at midnight and carried, dead and naked to that far-away city that she had always honoured with her Sunday's best; the place beside her family was to be empty till the crack of doom; her innocent and almost venerable members to be exposed to that last curiosity of the anatomist.

Late one afternoon the pair set forth, well wrapped in cloaks and furnished with a formidable bottle. It rained without remission—a cold, dense, lashing rain. Now and again there blew a puff of wind, but these sheets of falling water kept it down. Bottle and all, it was a sad and silent drive as far as Penicuik, where they were to spend the evening. They stopped once, to hide their implements in a thick bush not far from the churchyard, and once again at the Fisher's Tryst, to have a toast before the kitchen fire and vary their nips of whisky with a glass of ale. When they reached their journey's end the gig was housed, the horse was fed and comforted, and the two young doctors in a private room sat down to the best dinner and the best wine the house afforded. The lights, the fire, the beating rain upon the window, the cold, incongruous work that lay before them, added zest to their enjoyment of the meal. With every glass their cordiality increased. Soon

Macfarlane handed a little pile of gold to his companion.

"A compliment," he said. "Between friends these little d——d accommodations ought to fly like pipe-lights."

Fettes pocketed the money, and applauded the sentiment to the echo. "You are a philosopher," he cried. "I was an ass till I knew you. You and K—— between you, by the Lord Harry! but you'll make a man of me."

"Of course we shall," applauded Macfarlane. "A man? I tell you, it required a man to back me up the other morning. There are some big, brawling, forty-year-old cowards who would have turned sick at the look of the d——d thing; but not you—you kept your head. I watched you."

"Well, and why not?" Fettes thus vaunted himself. "It was no affair of mine. There was nothing to gain on the one side but disturbance, and on the other I could count on your gratitude, don't you see?" And he slapped his pocket till the gold pieces rang.

Macfarlane somehow felt a certain touch of alarm at these unpleasant words. He may have regretted that he had taught his young companion so successfully, but he had no time to interfere, for the other noisily continued in this boastful strain:

"The great thing is not to be afraid. Now, between you and me, I don't want to hang—that's practical; but for all cant, Macfarlane, I was born with a contempt. Hell, God, Devil, right, wrong, sin, crime, and all the old gallery of curiosities—they may frighten boys, but men of the world, like you and me, despise them. Here's to the memory of Gray!"

It was by this time growing somewhat late. The

gig, according to order, was brought round to the door
with both lamps brightly shining, and the young men
had to pay their bill and take the road. They announced that they were bound for Peebles, and drove
in that direction till they were clear of the last houses
of the town; then, extinguishing the lamps, returned
upon their course, and followed a by-road toward
Glencorse. There was no sound but that of their own
passage, and the incessant, strident pouring of the
rain. It was pitch dark; here and there a white gate or
a white stone in the well guided them for a short space
across the night; but for the most part it was at a foot
pace, and almost groping, that they picked their way
through that resonant blackness to their solemn and
isolated destination. In the sunken woods that traverse
the neighbourhood by the burying-ground the last
glimmer failed them, and it became necessary to kindle
a match and reillumine one of the lanterns of the gig.
Thus, under the dripping trees, and environed by
huge and moving shadows, they reached the scene of
their unhallowed labours.

They were both experienced in such affairs, and
powerful with the spade; and they had scarce been
twenty minutes at their task before they were re-
warded by a dull rattle on the coffin lid. At the same
moment Macfarlane, having hurt his hand upon a
stone, flung it carelessly above his head. The grave, in
which they now stood almost to the shoulders, was
close to the edge of the plateau of the graveyard; and
the gig lamp had been propped, the better to illumi-
nate their labours, against a tree, and on the immediate verge of the steep bank descending to the stream.
Chance had taken a sure aim with the stone. Then
came a clang of broken glass; night fell upon them;

sounds alternately dull and ringing announced the
bounding of the lantern down the bank, and its oc-
casional collision with the trees. A stone or two, which
it had dislodged in its descent, rattled behind it into
the profundities of the glen; and then silence, like
night, resumed its sway; and they might bend their
hearing to its utmost pitch, but naught was to be heard
except the rain, now marching to the wind, now steadily falling over miles of open country.

They were so nearly at an end of their abhorred
task that they judged it wisest to complete it in the
dark. The coffin was exhumed and broken open; the
body inserted in the dripping sack and carried between
them to the gig; one mounted to keep it in its place,
and the other, taking the horse by the mouth, groped
along by wall and bush until they reached the wider
road by the Fisher's Tryst. Here was a faint, diffused
radiancy, which they hailed like daylight; by that they
pushed the horse to a good pace and began to rattle
along merrily in the direction of the town.

They had both been wetted to the skin during their
operations, and now, as the gig jumped among the
deep ruts, the thing that stood propped between them
fell now upon one and now upon the other. At every
repetition of the horrid contact each instinctively repelled it with the greater haste; and the process, natural although it was, began to tell upon the nerves of
the companions. Macfarlane made some ill-favoured
jest about the farmer's wife, but it came hollowly from
his lips, and was allowed to drop in silence. Still their
unnatural burden bumped from side to side; and now
the head would be laid, as if in confidence, upon their
shoulders, and now the drenching sackcloth would flap
icily about their faces. A creeping chill began to possess

the soul of Fettes. He peered at the bundle, and it seemed somehow larger than at first. All over the country-side, and from every degree of distance, the farm dogs accompanied their passage with tragic ululations; and it grew and grew upon his mind that some unnatural miracle had been accomplished, that some nameless change had befallen the dead body, and that it was in fear of their unholy burden that the dogs were howling.

"For God's sake," said he, making a great effort to arrive at speech, "for God's sake, let's have a light!"

Seemingly Macfarlane was affected in the same direction; for, though he made no reply, he stopped the horse, passed the reins to his companion, got down, and proceeded to kindle the remaining lamp. They had by that time got no farther than the cross-road down to Auchenclinny. The rain still poured as though the deluge were returning, and it was no easy matter to make a light in such a world of wet and darkness. When at last the flickering blue flame had been transferred to the wick and began to expand and clarify, and shed a wide circle of misty brightness round the gig, it became possible for the two young men to see each other and the thing they had along with them. The rain had moulded the rough sacking to the outlines of the body underneath; the head was distinct from the trunk, the shoulders plainly modelled; something at once spectral and human riveted their eyes upon the ghastly comrade of their drive.

For some time Macfarlane stood motionless, holding up the lamp. A nameless dread was swathed, like a wet sheet, about the body, and tightened the white skin upon the face of Fettes; a fear that was meaning-

ROBERT LOUIS STEVENSON

less, a horror of what could not be, kept mounting to
his brain. Another beat of the watch, and he had
spoken. But his comrade forestalled him.

"That is not a woman," said Macfarlane, in a
hushed voice.

"It was a woman when we put her in," whispered
Fettes.

"Hold that lamp," said the other. "I must see her
face."

And as Fettes took the lamp his companion untied
the fastenings of the sack and drew down the cover
from the head. The light fell very clear upon the dark,
well-moulded features and smooth-shaven cheeks of a
too familiar countenance, often beheld in dreams of
both of these young men. A wild yell rang up into
the night; each leaped from his own side into the road-
way: the lamp fell, broke, and was extinguished; and
the horse, terrified by this unusual commotion, bounded
and went off toward Edinburgh at a gallop, bearing
along with it, sole occupant of the gig, the body of the
dead and long-dissected Gray.

Only the Guilty Run

He was grown up now and he would act grown up.

It was a few hours after dinner, that cool evening at the beginning of September. Charlie got up from the mauve stuffed chair in the living room and walked into the foyer, opened the closet and grabbed his red wool sweater from the hook. He said nothing to his parents and they said nothing to him. His mother had looked up from her sewing which was spread out in her lap, and smiled tentatively, and Charlie had winked in answer. His father had not taken his eyes from the ball game on the television screen. It was understood that they would not ask him where he was going or what time he would return. This was his sixteenth summer, and when the new term started at school, Charlie would be a senior. If he wanted to, he could even smoke in front of his family, and he had done so once. In July he had camped out for two weeks with four of his best buddies far up into the Adirondacks. His allowance was increased from two dollars and a half a week to fifteen dollars a month, and as long as he did not run short, he did not have to account for the money. After Labor Day he would go to work from four until eight in Allen's Pharmacy, and open a savings account in the bank where his father was a teller.

Charlie stood in the hallway of the apartment building and pushed the button of the self-operating elevator. Little Billy Crandell's mother was standing in front of 3C yelling, "C'mon now, Billy. It's after eight. Billy, I said hurry!" Billy was trudging up the stairs slowly, dragging his coat on the cement steps, his dark eyes sad, his lips pouting. He passed Charlie, and Charlie ruffled the boy's yellow hair and smiled to himself. He could remember when he was only eleven.

Downstairs in the lobby he paused before the large square mirror. He was tall, and not skinny any more. His shoulders were broad, and his legs and arms were muscular, firm. The deep tan gave his face a rugged, masculine look that set off his gray eyes and made his teeth seem very white when he grinned. The close-cropped haircut helped too. He looked older than he had in June. Even though it had only been three months, he *knew* he looked older—acted older too. He wasn't a kid any longer. He was grown up. He was on his own.

Then he thought of her. . . . Of course, he had never really stopped thinking of her. Not all summer. He had pretended to himself that she was not important, that she was merely a stage he had gone through, that it did not matter now. But in his heart he knew differently. It was crazy the way he had dreamed of her those days and nights during June, July, and August. In his sleep he would see her entering the classroom again, smiling with the dimples at her cheeks, her green eyes sparkling, the soft, long, flaxen-colored hair touching her shoulders. He had seen her that way countless times, but when he dreamed of it, he made it different. She called the roll the way she always did, but when she came to his name, she stopped and looked up, searching the room for him. Then, when their eyes met, a wistful expression came over her countenance. She said, "Oh, *there* you are," and the tone in her voice was hallowed and tender. What she was really saying was, "Charlie, Charlie, I've missed you *so!*"

He would wake up from that recurring dream feeling glorious. He would sing "I'll Be Seeing You" in the shower, shine his scuffed-up brown oxfords, and take long walks, humming to himself and watching the sky. It didn't matter that it was only a dream. It didn't matter that Miss Lattimore had never said anything of the kind to him. It was wonderful, wasn't it? He was in love with her. She was his high-school English teacher and she was probably past twenty-seven, and he was just sixteen—but that didn't matter either. Those mornings after the dream, he believed only in his love, in Jill—that was her name. Miss Jill Lattimore.

Sometimes he was depressed. He did not always sing or hum or smile or think it was wonderful to be alive. He read poetry—especially the plays and sonnets of Shakespeare—imitating the way she had read them aloud in class.

*How like a winter hath my absence
been,
From thee—*

That was the one he read most of the time, and he
would close the book, hold his head in his hands, and
say, "Jill!" and then, "Jill! If you only knew. . . ."
Charlie shook his head and stared at the mirror in
the lobby of his apartment house where he had been
standing, thinking of her. Suddenly he laughed and
said to the mirror, "Shakespeare! *Me* like Shakespeare? Ha!" He shrugged his shoulders the way Sid
Caesar might have done on television. "Yeah, *me*. Me
—Charlie Wright. I like Shakespeare, that's all. And
because of her!" He laughed again, but his stomach
did a flip, and when he walked out the door of the
building, he was frowning.

It was getting dark. There were some kids sitting
on the curb under the streetlight at the end of the
block. He began to walk in the opposite direction, up
the winding road of Overlook Terrace to Fort Washington Avenue. He had always liked living in Washington Heights. It was close to the river and the
George Washington Bridge, and he used to sit on the
low banks near the water and watch the tugs and
barges go by. Last year he had found another reason
for liking Washington Heights. Miss Lattimore lived
on Cabrini Boulevard, a few blocks from where
Charlie was walking right at that moment.

He had gone by the Excelsior Apartments dozens
of times, and once he had gone inside and read her
name on the mailbox. *Lattimore-4B*. Later, as he
stood in the road behind the building, he picked out her
apartment from all the others. It was in the rear, fac-

ing the Hudson. Sometimes in the early evening he would see the lights up there and wonder what she was doing. He would make a bet with himself. "If she comes to the window and looks out, she feels the same way I do." . . . But she never came to the window and Charlie went home sorrowfully, moping around in his bedroom, angry at his mother's questioning.

His mother would say, "Do you feel all right, dear?"

"Sure," Charlie answered, "swell!" He would say it very sarcastically.

"Darling, if anything's the matter . . ."

"Aw for Pete's sake," he would exclaim. "For Pete's sake, mom!"

Then before he went to bed he would go to his mother, pat her under the chin with his finger and say, "'Night, sweetheart. Pleasant dreams." Because he was always sorry when he was rude to her. When you came right down to it, he had a swell family. His mother and dad always played square with him, and he used to think, "Why, I can tell them anything—*anything!*" But he couldn't tell them about this. This was different. He was in love—desperately in love—with an older woman, and he had been in love with her for one whole year.

Even the fellows at school didn't know. He made sure of that. Some of the boys used to say, "Hey, that Lattimore is some chick, huh? All teachers should have *her* looks." Charlie would smirk and tell them they were loony. He cut up in her class, shot paper airplanes across the room, dropped aspirin in inkwells, and whistled "La Cucaracha" when she read poetry. One day she kept him after class.

"Charlie," she said, "why can't we get along?"

He wanted to cry right then and there.

He said, "What difference does it make!"

"It makes a great deal of difference to me," she answered quietly, "You know, Charlie, I've read your compositions carefully. I think we both know you don't act the way you feel inside. You're quite a sensitive young man, Charlie. You write beautifully about beautiful things."

He thought, if she doesn't stop saying my name that way I *will* cry; if she doesn't stop saying things like that I *will* cry—I just won't be able to help myself.

He said gruffly, "I'll be late for Latin."

"Please think it over," Miss Jill Lattimore said.

The truth was, she understood him and no one else really did. "*You're quite a sensitive young man, Charlie. You write beautifully about beautiful things.*" And what else had she said? That he didn't act the way he felt inside. He should have said, "Yes, Miss Lattimore. 'All the world's a stage, and all the men and women merely players.' " He should have said something adult and intellectual—like something Shakespeare had written. She was a bug on Shakespeare and Charlie was too now. He had thumbed through the pocket-book Shakespeare he kept under his pillow until the pages were worn and marked. . . .

This term it will be different, Charlie thought as he strolled along Fort Washington Avenue, past the drug store where the gang crowded in booths, listening to the juke box and drinking cokes. He didn't want to go in the drug store and hear all that kid talk. He wanted to be by himself and think about how different it would be this term. He was grown up now and he would act grown up. Jill would notice it immediately because he wasn't going to clown around any more.

The very first morning of class he would go to her and say, "You know, Miss Lattimore, I was something of a buffoon last year." Buffoon was a good word. And then he would quote, "My salad days, when I was green in judgement." That would do it. Short and to the point, with a peppering of Shakespeare and a sincere smile. He had been practicing sincere smiles all summer.

Charlie thought it was a lucky thing she taught both Junior and Senior English. He might never have seen her again, or heard her voice, or watched the proud way she walked with her head held high, the tilt to her nose giving her face a saucy look. He was a lot taller than she was, and really, when he thought about it, she seemed younger than he. It was a fact she didn't *look* twenty-seven—she didn't look that old at all.

There was a moon up over the Hudson and dots of light on the Jersey side. Charlie walked slowly and he made his hands into fists. He had not seen her for three months. He remembered she had said that she would spend the summer in Colorado with her folks. School began in three days and she should be back. He turned and walked down Cabrini Boulevard. "*How like a Winter hath my absense been, From thee.*"

He stopped before the building where she lived, and when he looked up, he saw the lights there. She was back! There was a drum in his stomach and he could feel his knees weaken. He did a strange thing. He kept walking toward the rear of the building until he could touch the brick with his hand. He touched it very gently. . . . When he saw the fire escape, he said in a whisper to himself, "Don't be crazy, Charlie. Hey, don't be crazy!"

It was easy because he wore sneakers on his feet and he went up the iron steps like a cat. He was afraid too. He had never done anything like this in his life and the moment had no reality for him. The moon was bright and big, and when he looked down he felt dizzy. He kept thinking "Go back"—but he wanted to see her.

He kept going until he came to the fourth level. At the windows of 4B he crouched, lifting his head slowly to stare into the room. She was not there. He saw the bookcases, the wide gray rug, the modern lamps and low tables, and the black vase of flowers. *Her* room. Her living room. He just kept looking at it, trying to imagine her there.

Then everything happened.

He remembered the sudden flash of light, the sound of a harsh voice ordering him to halt. He remembered running up the steps of the fire escape to the fifth floor and the sixth, his hands shaking, his legs like lead under him. He thought he would fall, he wished he could jump, and after he had gone three flights up, he stopped and held on to the wall of the building.

Two shots rang out in the night and he screamed, terrified. He stood clutching the brick, sobbing, saying "No!" aloud. A dark figure came stealthily toward him, grabbed the back of his sweater, jerked him forward. He felt the rough material of a policeman's coat. Again, he looked down and the scene made him dizzy. He felt himself buckle and the voice grew faint. . . .

"He's a good boy, a *good* boy," his mother was crying. Charlie sat slumped in the wooden chair at the

Police Station, hearing his mother defend him, his father question him. A fat Police Captain in shirt-sleeves stood next to Charlie, his face kindly, his eye dark and serious.

"Try to explain, son," Charlie's father said, "What made you go up there? Try to explain before Miss Lattimore comes."

Charlie couldn't answer. He kept thinking that he was very nearly killed.

"Were there any other boys with you?" the Captain asked. "We got a report saying there was only one."

"He's an Eagle Scout," his mother said to no one in particular. Her eyes were tired and red.

"Don't you like Miss Lattimore?" His father's tone was patient, soft. "Chuck, did you really go up there to look in *her* window?"

The officer interrupted. "That's where he was, all right—kneeling right outside her window."

Charlie knew he would cry out again any moment. There was a knot in his throat.

"I fired over his head," the officer said, "but it was dangerous just the same. He could have got it if he'd kept on running."

"What about it, Chuck?" his father said. "Try to tell us, son."

He had almost been shot down, Charlie thought, like a criminal. He was dreaming, he would wake up. . . .

When he heard Miss Lattimore's voice, his hands went cold. His lips quivered and he could not have spoken if he had wanted to. He sat shaking.

"He's a good boy," his mother repeated, and he

thought, "Aw mom, dear mom," and he kept his head lowered to keep them from seeing that his eyes were filled.

"I know he is," he heard Miss Lattimore say.

"We're sorry about this," his father apologized.

Charlie could not look up at her, and he could not stop his shoulders from heaving with the great sobs inside him. He was just a kid after all, he told himself, just a big sissy.

"I should have asked the janitor," Miss Lattimore began, "but I never thought he'd be hurt doing me that favor."

"You mean?" Charlie's mother cried out.

"My television wires. The nails were loose. It's attached to the window on the ledge outside and I didn't think he'd hurt himself. I certainly never thought he'd be reported for being a peeping Tom."

Then Charlie looked up. He stared at her. She looked little and delicate, standing there in the sky-blue linen dress with the sweater, the same color as her hair, over her shoulders.

"He was doing you a favor?" his mother asked hopefully.

"That's right," Miss Lattimore answered. "I met him on the Boulevard and asked him if he would. I just returned yesterday and there's so much work, getting resettled and—"

She's beautiful, he thought, she's like an angel.

"Well," the Captain boomed out, "that ends that!"

"Chuck, you should have said so." His father was smiling broadly, clasping his arm around Charlie's shoulder. "Good lord, son, you should have spoken up, told us about it."

Miss Lattimore was holding her glance steady with Charlie's. "He was probably afraid," she said carefully. "He could have been killed."

She had done this thing for him. She had understood, she had known, and she had done this thing for him. . . .

"Never run," the officer said at the door. "Only guilty people run, lad."

"Your post cards were forwarded to me, Charlie," Miss Lattimore said. "You seem to have had a nice summer." They were leaving the Police Station now —Miss Lattimore, Charlie, his mother and his father.

His mother said, "He went camping with some other boys alone in the woods. He's sixteen now, you know."

He didn't mind his mother saying that. For some reason he didn't mind.

His father said, "I have my car, Miss Lattimore. May I drop you?"

In the car everyone began to laugh about it. It wasn't really funny, his mother said, because he could have been killed. Charlie laughed too, sitting in the back seat looking at Jill's light blonde hair. When she waved goodbye to them in front of the Excelsior apartment house, Charlie watched her walk up the path until she was out of sight. Then he sat forward, resting his chin on the back of the seat where his parents sat, and he kept thinking about her. . . .

It was near midnight. He had waited for the house to be still, for the door to his parents room to close. Quickly and quietly he went down the hall, down the steps to the lobby, and out into the street. The late night air was colder now and he wished he had brought his topcoat, instead of wearing just his suit. His only suit—blue serge with a good press.

The streets were empty and the stores along Fort Washington Avenue were dark. When he came to Cabrini Boulevard, he did not turn down the back road. He walked directly to the entrance of the Excelsior. A man with a skinny dog on a leash held the door open for Charlie, and inside he took the elevator to the fourth floor.

When she answered the door, he said, "Hello, Jill."

She stood in a white terry-cloth robe, her long hair pulled behind her ears and held with a red ribbon. Her eyes were wide, her lips half parted, and she looked at him with disbelief.

"Aren't you going to ask me in?" he said.

She blocked the entrance. "Charlie Wright, go home. Now!"

"Jill," he said, "Listen, Jill—"

"Charlie, what on earth? Don't you realize that I was trying to be a good sport tonight? I was trying to help you, Charlie, don't you *realize* that?"

"Why?" he said. "Why were you helping me?" He made his lips grin playfully, but he was less sure now.

"You poor kid. Please, Charlie, go home! Don't you see—I was trying to help you because I knew you had a crush on me. All those post cards, and the ridiculous way you acted in my classes last year—and your compositions. Charlie, please! Don't make me do anything mean."

He didn't know what to do. He felt foolish standing before her in his best suit with his new shirt and striped tie, and the gold tie-clip his father had given him for his birthday. He said "Crush?" and his voice did not sound like his own.

"Charlie, leave right now. I mean it." Her eyes were round and as he looked at her intently, he suddenly became aware of something terrible. She was afraid of him. She was genuinely afraid of his presence there.

He said, "Look, I won't hurt you. I only want to— I want, I—" He began to stutter. He felt confused. He wanted to make it all right, to make whatever he was doing all right. She *wasn't* in love with him. He wanted to make that all right too, and it was. It was, because he didn't love her either any more. In those slow seconds he experienced a horrible awakening. All he wanted to do was go home, to get some sleep, to wake up and find the gang tomorrow. Play ball. Go up to the drug store. Things like that. He wasn't Charlie Wright standing before the door of his English teacher's apartment. That was crazy.

"Go on, now!" She raised her voice and the sound startled him. Now that he knew, he did not want anything more to happen to spoil it. He reached out without being conscious of what he was doing—only to stop the frantic words she was saying to him, to stop them and tell her he was sorry, that he was a fool, and was going.

He clamped his hand across her mouth. Instantly, she screamed. She screamed the way he had when they had shot at him on the fire escape.

He said, "Listen—I—" But it was too late. The man from the next apartment was running toward Charlie. Charlie stood still. Miss Jill Lattimore was crying, and the man had Charlie by the shoulder.

"Miss Lattimore," he tried to say again, but she

was sobbing her words hysterically now. She was telling the man that Charlie was a foolish kid with a crush on her, that she couldn't control him, that this time he had gone too far. . . . Charlie knew that in a matter of minutes the police would be on their way, the phone would ring out in the darkness of his parents' bedroom, and now he was on his own—really on his own.

◆

My Friend Paton

*His daughter was scarcely less a mystery than he, for,
though she went out as often as twice or thrice a
week, she was always closely veiled. . .*

Mathew Morriss, my father, was a cotton merchant in
Liverpool twenty-five years ago—a steady, laborious,
clear-headed man, very affectionate and genial in his
private intercourse. He was wealthy, and we lived in
a sumptuous house in the upper part of the city. This
was when I was about ten years old. My father was
twice married; I was the child of the first wife, who
died when I was very young; my stepmother came
five years later. She was the elder of two sisters, both
beautiful women. The sister often came to visit us. I
remember I liked her better than I liked my stepmother; in fact, I regarded her with that sort of
romantic attachment that often is developed in lads
of my age. She had golden brown hair and a remarkably sweet voice, and she sang and played in a manner

that transported me with delight; for I was already devoted to music. She was of a gentle yet impulsive temperament, easily moved to smiles and tears; she seemed to me the perfection of womankind, and I made no secret of my determination to marry her when I grew up. She used to caress me, and look at me in a dreamy way, and tell me I was the nicest and handsomest boy in the world. "And as soon as you are a year older than I am, John," she would say, "you shall marry me, if you like."

Another frequent visitor at our house at this time was not nearly so much a favorite of mine. This was a German, Adolf Körner by name, who had been a clerk in my father's concern for a number of years, and had just been admitted junior partner. My father placed every confidence in him, and often declared that he had the best idea of business he had ever met with. This may very likely have been the fact; but to me he appeared simply a tall, grave, taciturn man, of cold manners, speaking with a slight German accent, which I disliked. I suppose he was about thirty-seven years of age, but I always thought of him as older than my father, who was fifty. Another and more valid reason for my disliking Körner was that he was in the habit of paying a great deal of attention to my lady-love, Miss Juliet Tretherne. I used to upbraid Juliet about encouraging his advances, and I expressed my opinion of him in the plainest language, at which she would smile in a preoccupied way, and would sometimes draw me to her and kiss me on the forehead. Once she said, "Mr. Körner is a very noble gentleman; you must not dislike him." This had the effect of making me hate him all the more.

One day I noticed an unusual commotion in the

house, and Juliet came down-stairs attired in a lovely white dress, with a long veil, and fragrant flowers in her hair. She got into a carriage with my father and stepmother, and drove away. I did not understand what it meant, and no one told me. After they were gone I went into the drawing-room, and, greatly to my surprise, saw there a long table covered with a white cloth and laid out with a profusion of good things to eat and drink in sparkling dishes and decanters. In the middle of the table was a great cake covered with white frosting; the butler was arranging some flowers round it.

"What is that cake for, Curtis?" I asked.

"For the bride, to be sure," said Curtis, without looking up.

"The bride! who is she?" I demanded in astonishment.

"Your aunt Juliet, to be sure!" said Curtis, composedly, stepping back and contemplating his floral arrangement with his head on one side.

I asked no more, but betook myself with all speed to my room, locked the door, flung myself on the bed, and cried to heartbreaking with grief, indignation and mortification. After a very long time some one tried the door, and a voice—the voice of Juliet—called to me. I made no answer. She began to plead with me; I resisted as long as I could, but finally my affection got the better of my resentment, and I arose and opened the door, hiding my tear-stained face behind my arm. Juliet caught me in her arms and kissed me; tears were running down her own cheeks. How lovely she looked! My heart melted, and I was just on the point of forgiving her when the voice of Körner became audible from below, calling out "Mrs. Körner!"

I tore myself away from her, and cried passionately, "You don't love me! you love him! go to him!" She looked at me for a moment with a pained expression; then she put her hand in the pocket of her dress and drew out something done up in white paper. "See what I have brought you, you unkind boy," said she. "What is it?" I demanded. "A piece of my wedding-cake," she replied. "Give it me!" said I. She put it in my hand; I ran forward to the head of the stairs, which Körner was just ascending, dashed the cake in his face, and then rushed back to my own room, whence neither threats nor coaxing availed to draw me forth for the rest of the day.

I never saw Juliet again. She and her husband departed on their wedding-trip that afternoon; it was to take them as far as Germany, for Körner said that he wished to visit his father and mother, who were still alive, before settling down permanently in Liverpool. Whether they really did so was never discovered. But, about a fortnight later, a dreadful fact came to light. Körner—the grave and reticent Körner, whom everybody trusted and thought so highly of—was a thief, and he had gone off with more than half my father's property in his pocket. The blow almost destroyed my father, and my stepmother, too, for that matter, for at first it seemed as though Juliet must have been privy to the crime. This, however, turned out not to have been the case. Her fate must have been all the more terrible on that account; but no news of either of them ever came back to us, and my father would never take any measures to bring Körner to justice. It was several months before he recovered from the shock sufficiently to take up business again; and then the American Civil War came and completed his ruin.

He died, a poor and broken-down man, a year later. My stepmother, who was really an admirable woman, realized whatever property remained to us, took a small house, and sent me to an excellent school, where I was educated for Cambridge. Meanwhile I had been devoting all possible time to music; for I had determined to become a composer, and I was looking forward, after taking my degree, to completing my musical education abroad; but my mother's health was precarious, and, when the time came, she found herself unequal to making the journey, and the change of habits and surroundings that it implied. We lived very quietly in Liverpool for three or four years; then she died, and, after I had settled our affairs, I found myself in possession of a small income and alone in the world. Without loss of time I set out for the Continent.

I went to a German city, where the best musical training was to be had, and made my arrangements to pass several years there. At the banker's, when I went to provide for the regular receipt of my remittances, I met a young American, by name Paton Jeffries. He was from New England, and, I think, a native of the State of Connecticut; his father, he told me, was a distinguished inventor, who had made and lost a considerable fortune in devising a means of promoting sleep by electricity. Paton was studying to be an architect, which, he said, was the coming profession in his country; and it was evident, on a short acquaintance, that he was a fellow of unusual talents—one of those men of whom you say that, come what may, they are always sure to fall on their feet. For my part, I have certainly never met with so active and versatile a spirit. He was a year or so older than I, rather tall than short, lightly but strongly built, with a keen, smiling, subtle face, a finely-developed forehead, light wavy hair, and gray eyes, very penetrating and bright. There was a pleasing kind of eagerness and volubility in his manner of talking, and a slight imperfection, not amounting to a lisp, in his utterance, which imparted a naïve charm to his speech. He used expressive and rapid gestures with his hands and arms, and there was a magnetism, a fascination, about the whole man that strongly impressed me. I was at that period much more susceptible of impressions, and prone to yield to them, than I am now. Paton's rattling vivacity, his knowledge of the world, his entertaining talk and stories, his curiosity, enterprise, and audacity, took me by storm; he was my opposite in temperament and character, and it seemed to me that he had most of the advantages on his side. Nevertheless, he professed, and I still believe he felt, a great liking for me, and we speedily came to an agreement to seek a lodging together. On the second day of our search, we found just what we wanted.

It was an old house, on the outskirts of the town, standing by itself, with a small garden behind it. It had formerly been occupied by an Austrian baron, and it was probably not less than two hundred years old. The baron's family had died out, or been dispersed, and now the venerable edifice was let, in the German fashion, in separate floors or *étages,* communicating with a central staircase. Some alterations rendered necessary by this modification had been made, but substantially the house was unchanged. Our apartment comprised four or five rooms on the left of the landing and at the top of the house, which consisted of three stories. The chief room was the parlor, which looked down through a square bow-window on the street. This room was of irregular shape, one end being narrower than the other, and nearly fitting the space at this end was a kind of projecting shelf or mantelpiece (only, of course, there was no fireplace under it, open fireplaces being unknown in Germany), upon which rested an old cracked looking-glass, made in two compartments, the frame of which, black with age and fly-spots, was fastened against the wall. The shelf was supported by two pilasters; but the object of the whole structure was a mystery; so far as appeared, it served no purpose but to support the looking-glass, which might just as well have been suspended from a nail in the wall. Paton, I remember, betrayed a great deal of curiosity about it; and since the consideration of the problem was more in his line of business than in mine, I left it to him. At the opposite end of the room stood a tall earthenware stove. The walls were wainscoted five feet up from the dark polished floor, and were hung with several smoky old paintings, of no great artistic value. The chairs and tables were plain, but very heavy and solid, and of a dark hue like the room. The window was nearly as wide as it was high, and opened laterally from the center on hinges. The other rooms were of the same general appearance, but smaller. We both liked the place, and soon made ourselves very comfortable in it. I hired a piano, and had it conveyed upstairs to the parlor; while Paton disposed his architectural paraphernalia on and in the massive writing-table near the window. Our cooking and other household duties were done for us by the wife of the *portier,* the official corresponding to the French *concierge,* who, in all German houses, attends at the common door, and who, in this case, lived in a couple of musty little closets opening into the lower hall, and eked out his official salary by cobbling shoes. He was an odd, grotesque humorist, of most ungainly exterior, black haired and bearded, with a squint, a squab nose, and a short but very powerful figure. Dirty he was beyond belief, and he was abominably fragrant of vile tobacco. For my part, I could not endure this fellow; but Paton, who had much more of what he called human nature in him than I had, established friendly relations with him at once, and reported that he found him very amusing. It was characteristic of Paton that, though he knew much less about the German language than I did, he could understand and make himself understood in it much better; and, when we were in company, it was always he who did the talking.

It would never have occurred to me to wonder, much less to inquire, who might be the occupants of the other *étages;* but Paton was more enterprising, and before we had been settled three days in our new quarters, he had gathered from his friend the portier, and from other sources, all the obtainable information on the subject. The information was of no particular interest, however, except as regarded the persons who dwelt on the floor immediately below us. They were two—an old man and a young woman, supposed to be his daughter. They had been living here several years —from before the time, indeed, that the portier had occupied his present position. In all these years the old man was known to have been out of his room only twice. He was certainly an eccentric person, and was said to be a miser and extremely wealthy. The portier further averred that his property—except such small portion of it as was invested and on the income of

which he lived—was realized in the form of diamonds
and other precious stones, which, for greater security,
he always carried, waking or sleeping, in a small
leathern bag, fastened round his neck by a fine steel
chain. His daughter was scarcely less a mystery than
he, for, though she went out as often as twice or thrice
a week, she was always closely veiled, and her figure
was so disguised by the long cloak she wore that it was
impossible to say whether she were graceful or de-
formed, beautiful or ugly. The balance of belief, however, was against her being attractive in any respect.
The name by which the old miser was known was
Kragendorf; but, as the portier sagaciously remarked,
there was no knowing, in such cases, whether the name
a man bore was his own or somebody's else.

This Kragendorf mystery was another source of
apparently inexhaustible interest to Paton, who was
fertile in suggestions as to how it might be explained
or penetrated. I believe he and the portier talked it
over at great length, but, so far as I am aware, without
arriving at any solution. I took little heed of the
matter, being now fully absorbed in my studies; and
it is to be hoped that Herr Kragendorf was not of a
nervous temperament, otherwise he must have in-
veighed profanely against the constant piano-practice
that went on over his head. I also had a violin, on
which I flattered myself I could perform with a good
deal of expression, and by and by, in the long, still
evenings—it was November, but the temperature was
still mild—I got into the habit of strolling along the
less frequented streets, with my violin under my shoulder, drawing from it whatever music my heart desired. Occasionally I would pause at some convenient
spot, lean against a wall, and give myself up to im-

provisation. At such times a little cluster of auditors would gradually collect in front of me, listening for the most part silently, or occasionally giving vent to low grunts and interjections of approval. One evening, I remember, a young woman joined the group, though keeping somewhat in the background; she listened intently, and after a time gradually turned her face toward me, unconsciously as it were; and the light of a street-lamp at a little distance revealed a countenance youthful, pale, sad, and exquisitely beautiful. It impressed me as with a vague reminiscence of something I had seen or imagined—some pictured face, perhaps, caught in a glance and never to be identified. Her eyes finally met mine; I stopped playing. She started, gave me an alarmed look, and, gliding swiftly away, disappeared. I could not forget this incident; it haunted me strangely and persistently. Many a time thereafter I revisited the same spot, and drew together other audiences, but the delicate girl with the dark-blue eyes and the tender, sensitive mouth, was never again among them.

It was at this epoch, I think, that the inexhaustible Paton made a discovery. From my point of view it was not a discovery of any moment; but, as usual, he took interest in it enough for both of us. It appeared that, in attempting to doctor the crack in the old looking-glass, a large piece of the plate had got loose, and come away in his hands; and in the space behind he had detected a paper, carefully folded and tied up with a piece of faded ribbon. Paton was never in the habit of hampering himself with fine-drawn scruples, and he had no hesitation in opening the folded paper and spreading it out on the table. Judging from the glance I gave it, it seemed to be a confused and abstruse mixture of irregular geometrical figures and cramped German chirography. But Paton set to work upon it with as much concentration as if it had been a recipe for the Philosopher's Stone; he reproduced the lines and angles on fresh paper, and labored over the writing with a magnifying-glass and a dictionary. At times he would mutter indistinctly to himself, lift his eyebrows, nod or shake his head, bite his lips, and rub his forehead, and anon fall to work again with fresh vigor. At last he leaned back in his chair, thumped his hand on the table, and laughed.

"Got it!" he exclaimed. "Say, John, old boy, I've got it! and it's the most curious old thing ever you saw in your life!"

"Something in analytical geometry, isn't it?" said I, turning round on my piano-stool.

"Analytical pudding's end! It's a plan of a house, my boy, and, what's more, of this very house we're in! That's a find, and no mistake! These are the descriptions and explanations—these bits of writing. It's a perfect labyrinth of Crete! Udolpho was nothing to it!"

"Well, I suppose it isn't of much value except as a curiosity?"

"Don't be too sure of that, John, my boy! Who knows but there's a treasure concealed somewhere in this house? or a skeleton in a secret chamber! This old paper may make our fortune yet!"

"The treasure wouldn't belong to us if we found it; and, besides, we can't make explorations beyond our own premises, and we know what's in them already."

"Do we? Did we know what was behind the looking-glass? Did you never hear of sliding panels, and private passages, and concealed staircases? Where's

your imagination, man? But you don't need imagination
—here it is in black and white!"

As he spoke, he pointed to a part of the plan; but,
as I was stooping to examine it, he seemed to change
his mind.

"No matter," he exclaimed, suddenly folding up the
paper and rising from his chair. "You're not an architect, and you can't be expected to go in for these things.
No; there's no practical use in it, of course. But secret
passages were always a hobby of mine. Well, what
are you going to do this evening? Come over to the
café and have a game of billiards!"

"No; I shall go to bed early to-night."

"You sleep too much," said Paton. "Everybody
does. If my father, instead of inventing a way of
promoting sleep, had invented a way of doing without
it, he'd have been the richest man in America to-day.
However, do as you like. I shan't be back till late."

He put on his hat and sallied forth with a cigar
in his mouth. Paton was of rather a convivial turn; he
liked to have a good time, as he called it; and, indeed,
he seemed to think that the chief end of man was to
get money enough to have a good time continually, a
sort of good eternity. His head was strong, and he
could stand a great deal of liquor; and I have seen
him sip and savor a glass of raw brandy or whisky as
another man would a glass of Madeira. In this, and
the other phases of his life about town, I had no par-
ticipation, being constitutionally as well as by training
averse therefrom; and he, on the other hand, would
never have listened to my sage advice to modify his
loose habits. Our companionship was apart from these
things; and, as I have said, I found in him a good deal

that I could sympathize with, without approaching the moralities.

That night, after I had been for some time alseep, I awoke and found myself listening to a scratching and shoving noise that seemed quite unaccountable. By-and-by it made me uneasy. I got up and went toward the parlor, from which the noise proceeded. On reaching the doorway, I saw Paton on his knees before one of the pilasters in the narrow end of the room; a candle was on the floor beside him, and he was busily at work at something, though what it was I could not make out. The creak of the threshold under my foot caused him to look round. He started violently, and sprang to his feet.

"Oh! it's you, is it?" he said, after a moment. "Great Scott! how you scared me! I was—I dropped a bit of money hereabouts, and I was scraping about to find it. No matter—it wasn't much! Sorry I disturbed you, old boy." And, laughing, he picked up his candle and went into his own room.

From this time there was a change vaguely perceptible in our mutual relations; we chatted together less than before, and did not see so much of each other. Paton was apt to be out when I was at home, and generally sat up after I was abed. He seemed to be busy about something—something connected with his profession, I judged; but, contrary to his former custom, he made no attempt to interest me in it. To tell the truth, I had begun to realize that our different tastes and pursuits must lead us further and further apart, and that our separation could be only a question of time. Paton was a materialist, and inclined to challenge all the laws and convictions that mankind has instituted and adopted; there was no limit to his radicalism. For example, on coming in one day, I found him with a curious antique poniard in his hands, which he had probably bought in some old curiosity shop. At first I fancied he meant to conceal it; but, if so, he changed his mind.

"What do you think of that?" he said, holding it out to me. "There's a solution of continuity for you! Mind you don't prick yourself! It's poisoned up to the hilt!"

"What do you want of such a thing?" I asked.

"Well, killing began with Cain, and isn't likely to go out of fashion in our day. I might find it convenient to give one of my friends—you, for instance—a reminder of his mortality some time. You'll say murder is immoral. Bless you, man, we never could do without it! No man dies before his time, and some one dies every day that some one else may live."

This was said in a jocose way, and, of course, Paton did not mean it. But it affected me unpleasantly nevertheless.

As I was washing my hands in my room, I happened to look out of my window, which commanded a view of the garden at the back of the house. It was an hour after sunset, and the garden was nearly dark; but I caught a movement of something below, and, looking more closely, I recognized the ugly figure of the portier. He seemed to be tying something to the end of a long slender pole, like a gigantic fishing-rod; and presently he advanced beneath my window, and raised the pole as high as it would go against the wall of the house. The point he touched was the sill of the window below mine—probably that of the bedroom of Herr Kragendorf. At this juncture the portier seemed to be startled at something—possibly he saw me at my window; at all events, he lowered his pole and disappeared in the house.

The next day Paton made an announcement that took me by surprise. He said he had made up his mind to quit Germany, and that very shortly. He mentioned having received letters from home, and declared he had got, or should soon have got, all he wanted out of this country. "I'm going to stop paying money for instruction," he said, "and begin to earn it by work. I shall stay another week, but then I'm off. Too slow here for me! I want to be in the midst of things, using my time."

I did not attempt to dissuade him; in fact, my first feeling was rather one of relief; and this Paton, with his quick preceptions, was probably aware of.

"Own up, old boy!" he said, laughing; "you'll be able to endure my absence. And yet you needn't think of me as worse than anybody else. If everybody were musicians and moralists, it would be nice, no doubt; but one might get tired of it in time, and then what would you do? You must give the scamps and adventurers their innings, after all! They may not do much good, but they give the other fellows occupation. I was born without my leave being asked, and I may act as suits me without asking anybody's leave."

This was said on a certain bright morning after our first fall of snow; the tiled roofs of the houses were whitened with it, it cushioned the window-sills, and spread a sparkling blankness over the garden. In the streets it was already melting, and people were slipping and splashing on the wet and glistening pavements. After gazing out at this scene for a while, in a mood of unwonted thoughtfulness, Paton yawned, stretched himself, and declared his intention of taking a stroll before dinner. Accordingly he lit a cigar and went forth. I watched him go down the street and turn the corner.

An hour afterward, just when dinner was on the table, I heard an unusual noise and shuffling on the stairs, and a heavy knock on the door. I opened it, and saw four men bearing on a pallet the form of my friend Paton. A police officer accompanied them. They brought Paton in, and laid him on his bed. The officer told me briefly what had happened, gave me certain directions, and, saying that a surgeon would arrive immediately, he departed with the four men tramping behind him.

Paton had slipped in going across the street, and a tramway car had run over him. He was not dead, though almost speechless; but his injuries were such that it was impossible that he should recover. He kept his eyes upon me; they were as bright as ever, though his face was deadly pale. He seemed to be trying to read my thoughts—to find out my feeling about him, and my opinion of his condition. I was terribly shocked and grieved, and my face no doubt showed it. By-and-by I saw his lips move, and bent down to listen.

"Confounded nuisance!" he whispered faintly in my ear. "It's all right, though; I'm not going to die this time. I've got something to do, and I'm going to do it—devil take me if I don't!"

He was unable to say more, and soon after the surgeon came in. He made an examination, and it was evident that he had no hope. His shrug of the shoulders was not lost upon Paton, who frowned, and made a defiant movement of the lip. But presently he said to me, still in the same whisper, "John, if that old fool should be right—he won't be, but in case of accidents —you must take charge of my things—the papers, and all. I'll make you heir of my expectations! Write out a declaration to that effect: I can sign my name; and he'll be witness."

I did as he directed, and having explained to the surgeon the nature of the document, I put the pen in Paton's hand; but was obliged to guide his hand with my own in order to make an intelligible signature. The surgeon signed below, and Paton seemed satisfied. He closed his eyes; his sufferings appeared to be very slight. But, even while I was looking at him, a change came over his face—a deadly change. His eyes opened; they were no longer bright, but sunken and dull. He gave me a dusky look—whether of rage, of fear, or of entreaty, I could not tell. His lips parted, and a voice made itself audible; not like his own voice, but husky and discordant. "I'm going," it said. "But look out for me. . . . Do it yourself!"

"Der Herr ist todt" (the man is dead), said the surgeon the next minute.

It was true. Paton had gone out of this life at an hour's warning. What purpose or desire his last words indicated, there was nothing to show. He was dead; and yet I could hardly believe that it was so. He had been so much alive; so full of schemes and enterprises. Nothing now was left but that crushed and haggard figure, stiffening on the bed; nothing, at least, that mortal senses could take cognizance of. It was a strange thought.

Paton's funeral took place a few days afterward.

I returned from the graveyard weary in body and mind. At the door of the house stood the portier, who nodded to me, and said,

"A very sad thing to happen, worthy sir; but so it is in the world. Of all the occupants of this house, one would have said the one least likely to be dead to-day was Herr Jeffries. Heh! if I had been the good Providence, I would have made away with the old gentleman of the *étage* below, who is of no use to anybody."

This, for lack of a better, was Paton's funeral oration. I climbed the three flights of stairs and let myself into our apartment—mine exclusively now. The place was terribly lonely; much more so than if Paton had been alive anywhere in the world. But he was dead; and, if his own philosophy were true, he was annihilated. But it was not true! How distinct and minute was my recollection of him—his look, his gestures, the tones of his voice. I could almost see him before me; my memory of him dead seemed clearer than when he was alive. In that invisible world of the mind was he not living still, and perhaps not far away?

I sat down at the table where he had been wont to work, and unlocked the drawers in which he kept his papers. These, or some of them, I took out and spread before me. But I found it impossible, as yet, to concentrate my attention upon them; I pushed back my chair, and, rising, went to the piano. Here I remained for perhaps a couple of hours, striking the vague chords that echo wandering thoughts. I was trying to banish this haunting image of Paton from my mind, and at length I partly succeeded.

All at once, however, the impression of him (as

I may call it) came back with a force and vividness that startled me. I stopped playing, and sat for a minute perfectly still. I felt that Paton was in the room; that if I looked round I should see him. I however restrained myself from looking round with all the strength of my will—wherefore I know not. What I felt was not fear, but the conviction that I was on the brink of a fearful and unprecedented experience —an experience that would not leave me as it found me. This strange struggle with myself taxed all my powers; the sweat started out on my forehead. At last the moment came when I could struggle no longer. I laid my hand on the keyboard, and pushed myself round on the stool. There was a momentary dazzle before my eyes, and after that I saw plainly. My hand, striking the keys, had produced a jarring discord; and while this was yet tingling in my ears, Paton, who was sitting in his old place at the table, with his back toward me, faced about in his chair, and his eyes met mine. I thought he smiled.

My excitement was past, and was succeeded by a dead calm. I examined him critically. His appearance was much the same as when in life; nay, he was even more like himself than before. The subtle or crafty expression which had always been discernible in his features was now intensified, and there was something wild and covertly fierce in the shining of his gray eyes, something that his smile was unable to disguise. What was human and genial in my former friend had passed away, and what remained was evil—the kind of evil that I now perceived to have been at the base of his nature. It was a revelation of character terrible in its naked completeness. I knew at a glance that Paton must always have been a far more wicked man than I had ever imagined; and in his present state all the remains of goodness had been stripped away, and nothing but wickedness was left.

I felt impelled, by an impulse for which I could not account, to approach the table and examine the papers once more; and now it entered into my mind to perceive a certain method and meaning in them that had been hidden from me before. It was as though I were looking at them through Paton's intelligence, and with his memory. He had in some way ceased to be visible to me; but I became aware that he wished me to sit down in his chair, and I did so. Under his guidance, and in obedience to a will that seemed to be my own, and yet was in direct opposition to my real will, I began a systematic study of the papers. Paton, meanwhile, remained close to me, though I could no longer see him; but I felt the gaze of his fierce, shining eyes, and his crafty, evil smile. I soon obtained a tolerable insight into what the papers meant, and what was the scheme in which Paton had been so much absorbed at the time of his death, and which he had been so loath to abandon. It was a wicked and cruel scheme, worked out to the smallest particular. But, though I understood its hideousness intellectually, it aroused in me no corresponding emotion; my sensitiveness to right and wrong seemed stupefied or inoperative. I could say, "This is wicked," but I could not awaken in myself a horror of committing the wickedness; and, moreover, I knew that, if the influence Paton was able to exercise over me continued, I must in due time commit it.

Presently I became aware, or, to speak more accurately, I seemed to remember, that there was something in Paton's room which it was incumbent on me to procure. I went thither, lifted up a corner of the rug between the bed and the stove, and beheld, in an aperture in the floor, of the existence of which I had till now known nothing, the antique poisoned dagger that Paton had showed me a few weeks before, and which I had not seen since then. I brought it back to the sitting-room, put it in a drawer of the table, and locked the drawer, at the same time making a mental note to the effect that I should reopen the drawer at a certain hour of the night and take the dagger out. All this while Paton was close at hand, though not visible to sight; but I had a sort of inner perception of his presence and movements. All at once, at about the hour of sunset, I saw him again; he moved toward the looking-glass at the narrow end of the room, laid his hand upon one of the pilasters, glanced at me over his shoulder, and immediately seemed to stoop down. As I sat, the edge of the table hid him from sight. I stood up and looked across. He was not there; and a kind of reaction of my nerves informed me that he was gone absolutely, for the time.

This reaction produced a lassitude impossible to describe; it was overpowering, and I had no choice but to yield to it. I dropped back in my chair, leaned forward on the table, and instantly fell into a heavy sleep, or stupor.

I awoke abruptly, with a sensation as if a hand had been laid on my shoulder. It was night, and I knew that the hour I had noted in my mind was at hand. I opened the drawer and took out the dagger, which I put in my pocket. The house was quite silent. A shiver passed through me. I was aware that Paton was standing at the narrow end of the room, waiting for me: Yes—there he was, or the impression of him in my brain—what did it matter? I arose mechanically and walked toward him. He had no need to direct me: I knew all there was to do, and how to do it. I knelt on the floor, laid my shoulder against the pilaster, and pushed it laterally. It moved aside on a pivot, disclosing an iron ring let into the floor. I laid hold of this ring, and lifted. A section of the floor came up, and I saw a sort of ladder descending perpendicularly into darkness. Down the ladder Paton went, and I followed him. Arrived at the bottom, I turned to the left, led by an instinct or a fascination; passed along a passage barely wide enough to admit me, until I came against a smooth, hard surface. I passed my hand over it until I touched a knob or catch, which I pressed, and the surface gave way before me like a door. I stumbled forward, and found myself in a room of what was doubtless Herr Kragendorf's apartment. A keen, cold air smote against my face; and with it came a sudden influx of strength and self-possession. I felt that, for a moment at least, the fatal influence of Paton upon me was broken. But what was that sound of a struggle —those cries and gasps, that seemed to come from an adjoining room?

I sprang forward, opened a door, and beheld a tall old man, with white hair and beard, in the grasp of a ruffian whom I at once recognized as the portier. A broken window showed how he had effected his entrance. One hand held the old man by the throat; in the other was a knife, which he was prevented from using by a young woman, who had flung herself upon him in such a way as to trammel his movements. In another moment, however, he would have shaken her off.

But that moment was not allowed him. I seized

him with a strength that amazed myself—a strength which never came upon me before or since. The conflict lasted but a breath or two; I hurled him to the floor, and, as he fell, his right arm was doubled under him, and the knife which he held entered his back beneath the left shoulder-blade. When I rose up from the whirl and fury of the struggle, I saw the old man reclining exhausted on the bosom of the girl. I knew him, despite his white hair and beard. And the face that bent so lovingly above him was the face that had looked into mine that night on the street—the face of the blue-eyed maiden—of a younger and a lovelier Juliet! As I gazed, there came a thundering summons at the door, and the police entered.

My poor uncle Körner had not prospered after his great stroke of roguery. His wife had died of a broken heart, after giving birth to a daughter, and his stolen riches had vanished almost as rapidly as they were acquired. He had at last settled down with his daughter in this old house. The treasure in the leathern bag, though a treasure to him, was not of a nature to excite general cupidity. It consisted, not of precious stones, but of relics of his dead wife—her rings, a lock of her hair, her letters, a miniature of her in a gold case. These poor keepsakes, and his daughter, had been the only solace of his lonely and remorseful life.

It was uncertain whether Paton and the portier had planned the robbery together, or separately, and in ignorance of each other's purpose. Nor can I tell whether my disembodied visitor came to me with good or with evil intent. Wicked spirits, even when they seem to have power to carry out their purposes, are perhaps only permitted to do so, so far as is consistent with an overruling good of which they know nothing. Certainly, if I had not descended the secret passage, Körner would have been killed, and perhaps my Juliet likewise—the mother of my children. But should I have been led on to stab him myself, with the poisoned dagger, had the portier not been there? Juliet smiles and says No, and I am glad to agree with her. But I have never since then found that anniversary upon me, without a shudder of awe, and a dark thought of Paton Jeffries.

Playmates

He heard Monica whisper: "Mary! Elsie! Come on. It's all right. He's gone now."

I

Although everybody who knew Stephen Everton agreed that he was the last man under Heaven who ought to have been allowed to bring up a child, it was fortunate for Monica that she fell into his hands; else she had probably starved or drifted into some refuge for waifs and strays. True her father, Sebastian Threlfall the poet, had plenty of casual friends. Almost everybody knew him slightly, and right up to the time of his fatal attack of *delirium tremens* he contrived to look one of the most interesting of the regular frequenters of the Café Royal. But people are generally not hasty to bring up the children of casual acquaintances, particularly when such children may be suspected of having inherited more than a fair share of human weaknesses.

Of Monica's mother literally nothing was known. Nobody seemed able to say if she were dead or alive. Probably she had long since deserted Threlfall for some consort able and willing to provide regular meals.

Everton knew Threlfall no better than a hundred others knew him, and was ignorant of his daughter's existence until the father's death was a new topic of conversation in literary and artistic circles. People vaguely wondered what would become of "the kid"; and while they were still wondering, Everton quietly took possession of her.

Who's Who will tell you the year of Everton's birth, the names of his *Almae Matres* (Winchester and Magdalen College, Oxford), the titles of his books and of his predelictions for skating and mountaineering; but it is necessary to know the man a little less superficially. He was then a year or two short of fifty and looked ten years older. He was a tall, lean man, with a delicate pink complexion, an oval head, a Roman nose, blue eyes which looked out mildly through strong glasses, and thin straight lips drawn tightly over slightly protruding teeth. His high forehead was bare, for he was bald to the base of his skull. What remained of his hair was a neutral tint between black and grey, and was kept closely cropped. He contrived to look at once prim and irascible, scholarly and acute; Sherlock Holmes, perhaps, with a touch of old-maidishness.

The world knew him for a writer of books on historical crises. They were cumbersome books with cumbersome titles, written by a scholar for scholars. They brought him fame and not a little money. The money he could have afforded to be without, since he was modestly wealthy by inheritance. He was essentially a cold-blooded animal, a bachelor, a man of

152

regular and temperate habits, fastidious, and fond of quietude and simple comforts.

Nobody is ever likely to know why Everton adopted the orphan daughter of a man whom he knew but slightly and neither liked nor respected. He was no lover of children, and his humours were sardonic rather than sentimental. I am only hazarding a guess when I suggest that, like so many childless men, he had theories of his own concerning the upbringing of children, which he wanted to see tested. Certain it is that Monica's childhood, which had been extraordinary enough before, passed from the tragic to the grotesque.

Everton took Monica from the Bloomsbury "apartments" house, where the landlady, already nursing a bad debt, was wondering how to dispose of the child. Monica was then eight years old, and a woman of the world in her small way. She had lived with drink and poverty and squalor; had never played a game nor had a playmate; had seen nothing but the seamy side of life; and had learned skill in practising her father's petty shifts and mean contrivances. She was grave and sullen and plain and pale, this child who had never known childhood. When she spoke, which was as seldom as possible, her voice was hard and gruff. She was, poor little thing, as unattractive as her life could have made her.

She went with Everton without question or demur. She would no more have questioned anybody's ownership than if she had been an inanimate piece of luggage left in a cloak-room. She had belonged to her father. Now that he was gone to his own place she was the property of whomsoever chose to claim her. Everton took her with a cold kindness in which was neither love nor pity; in return she gave him neither love nor gratitude, but did as she was desired after the manner of a paid servant.

Everton disliked modern children, and for what he disliked in them he blamed modern schools. It may have been on this account that he did not send Monica to one; or perhaps he wanted to see how a child would contrive its own education. Monica could already read and write and, thus equipped, she had the run of his large library, in which was almost every conceivable kind of book from heavy tomes on abstruse subjects to trashy modern novels bought and left there by Miss Gribbin. Everton barred nothing, recommended nothing, but watched the tree grow naturally, untended and unpruned.

Miss Gribbin was Everton's secretary. She was the kind of hatchet-faced, flat-chested, middle-aged sexless woman who could safely share the home of a bachelor without either of them being troubled by the tongue of Scandal. To her duties was now added the instruction of Monica in certain elementary subjects. Thus Monica learned that a man named William the Conqueror arrived in England in 1066; but to find out what manner of man this William was, she had to go to the library and read the conflicting accounts of him given by the several historians. From Miss Gribbin she learned bare irrefutable facts; for the rest she was left to fend for herself. In the library she found herself surrounded by all the realms of reality and fancy, each with its door invitingly ajar.

Monica was fond of reading. It was, indeed, almost her only recreation, for Everton knew no other children of her age, and treated her as a grown-up member of the household. Thus she read everything from translations of the *Iliad* to Hans Andersen, from the

Bible to the love-gush of the modern female fiction-mongers.

Everton, although he watched her closely, and plied her with innocent-sounding questions, was never allowed a peep into her mind. What muddled dreams she may have had of a strange world surrounding the Hampstead house—a world of gods and fairies and demons, and strong silent men making love to sloppy-minded young women—she kept to herself. Reticence was all that she had in common with normal childhood, and Everton noticed that she never played.

Unlike most young animals, she did not take naturally to playing. Perhaps the instinct had been beaten out of her by the realities of life while her father was alive. Most lonely children improvise their own games and provide themselves with a vast store of make-believe. But Monica, as sullen-seeming as a caged animal, devoid alike of the naughtiness and the charms of childhood, rarely crying and still more rarely laughing, moved about the house sedate to the verge of being wooden. Occasionally Everton, the experimentalist, had twinges of conscience and grew half afraid. . . .

II

When Monica was twelve Everton moved his establishment from Hampstead to a house remotely situated in the middle of Suffolk, which was part of a recent legacy. It was a tall, rectangular Queen Anne house standing on a knoll above mashy fields and wind-bowed beech woods. Once it had been the manor house, but now little land went with it. A short drive passed between rank evergreens from the heavy wrought-iron gate to a circle of grass and flower beds in front of the house. Behind was an acre and a half of rank garden, given over to weeds and marigolds. The rooms were high and well lighted, but the house wore an air of depression as if it were a live thing unable to shake off some ancient fit of melancholy.

Everton went to live in the house for a variety of reasons. For the most part of a year he had been trying in vain to let or sell it, and it was when he found that he would have no difficulty in disposing of his house at Hampstead that he made up his mind. The old house, a mile distant from a remote Suffolk village, would give him all the solitude he required. Moreover he was anxious about his health—his nervous system had never been strong—and his doctor had recommended the bracing air of East Anglia.

He was not in the least concerned to find that the house was too big for him. His furniture filled the same number of rooms as it had filled at Hampstead, and the others he left empty. Nor did he increase his staff of three indoor servants and gardener. Miss Gribbin, now less dispensable than ever, accompanied him; and with them came Monica to see another aspect of life, with the same wooden stoicism which Everton had remarked in her upon the occasion of their first meeting.

As regarded Monica, Miss Gribbin's duties were then becoming more and more of a sinecure. "Lessons" now occupied no more than half an hour a day. The older Monica grew, the better she was able to grub for her education in the great library. Between Monica and Miss Gribbin there was neither love nor sympathy, nor was there any affectation of either. In their common duty to Everton they owed and paid certain duties to each other. Their intercourse began and ended there.

Everton and Miss Gribbin both liked the house at first. It suited the two temperaments which were alike in their lack of festivity. Asked if she too liked it, Monica said simply "Yes," in a tone which implied stolid and complete indifference.

All three in their several ways led much the same lives as they had led at Hampstead. But a slow change began to work in Monica, a change so slight and subtle that weeks passed before Everton or Miss Gribbin noticed it. It was late on an afternoon in early spring when Everton first became aware of something unusual in Monica's demeanor.

He had been searching in the library for one of his own books—*The Fall of the Commonwealth of England*—and having failed to find it went in search of Miss Gribbin and met Monica instead at the foot of the long oak staircase. Of her he casually inquired about the book, and she jerked up her head brightly, to answer him with an unwonted smile:

"Yes, I've been reading it. I expect I left it in the schoolroom. I'll go and see."

It was a long speech for her to have uttered, but Everton scarcely noticed that at the time. His attention was directed elsewhere.

"*Where* did you leave it?" he demanded.

"In the schoolroom," she repeated.

"I know of no schoolroom," said Everton coldly. He hated to hear anything mis-called, even were it only a room. "Miss Gribbin generally takes you for your lessons in either the library or the dining-room. If it is one of those rooms, kindly call it by its proper name."

Monica shook her head.

"No, I mean the schoolroom—the big empty room next to the library. That's what it's called."

Everton knew the room. It faced north, and seemed darker and more dismal than any other room in the house. He had wondered idly why Monica chose to spend so much of her time in a room bare of furniture, with nothing better to sit on than uncovered boards or a cushionless window-seat; and put it down to her genius for being unlike anybody else.

"Who calls it that?" he demanded.

"*It's* its name," said Monica smiling.

She ran upstairs, and presently returned with the book, which she handed to him with another smile. He was already wondering at her. It was surprising and pleasant to see her run, instead of the heavy and clumsy walk which generally moved her when she went to obey a behest. And she had smiled two or three times in the short space of a minute. Then he realized that for some little while she had been a brighter, happier creature than she had ever been at Hampstead.

"How did you come to call that room the schoolroom?" he asked, as he took the book from her hand.

"It *is* the schoolroom," she insisted, seeking to cover her evasion by laying stress on the verb.

That was all he could get out of her. As he questioned further the smiles ceased and the pale, plain little face became devoid of any expression. He knew then that it was useless to press her, but his curiosity was aroused. He inquired of Miss Gribbin and the servant, and learned that nobody was in the habit of calling the long, empty apartment the schoolroom.

Clearly Monica had given it its name. But why? She was so altogether remote from school and schoolrooms. Some germ of imagination was active in her small mind. Everton's interest was stimulated. He was like a doctor who remarks in a patient some abnormal symptom.

"Monica seems a lot brighter and more alert than she used to be," he remarked to Miss Gribbin.

"Yes," agreed the secretary. "I have noticed that. She is learning to play."

"To play what? The piano?"

"No, no. To play childish games. Haven't you heard her dancing about and singing?"

Everton shook his head and looked interested.

"I have not," he said. "Possibly my presence acts as a check upon her—er—exuberance."

"I hear her in that empty room which she insists upon calling the schoolroom. She stops when she hears my step. Of course, I have not interfered with her in any way, but I could wish that she would not talk to herself. I don't like people who do that. It is somehow —uncomfortable."

"I didn't know she did," said Everton slowly.

"Oh, yes, quite long conversations. I haven't actually heard what she talks about, but sometimes you would think she was in the midst of a circle of friends."

"In that same room?"

"Generally," said Miss Gribbin, with a nod.

Everton regarded his secretary with a slow, thoughtful smile.

"Development," he said, "is always extremely interesting. I am glad the place seems to suit Monica. I think it suits all of us."

There was a doubtful note in his voice as he uttered the last words, and Miss Gribbin agreed with him with the same lack of conviction in her tone. As a fact, Everton had been doubtful of late if his health had been benefited by the move from Hampstead. For the first week or two his nerves had been the better for the change of air; but now he was conscious of the beginning of a relapse. His imagination was beginning to play him tricks, filling his mind with vague, distorted fancies. Sometimes when he sat up late, writing—he was given to working at night on strong coffee—he became a victim of the most distressing nervous symptoms, hard to analyze and impossible to combat, which invariably drove him to bed with a sense of defeat.

That same night he suffered one of the variations of this common experience.

It was close upon midnight when he felt stealing over him a sense of discomfort which he was compelled to classify as fear. He was working in a small room leading out of the drawing-room which he had selected for his study. At first he was scarcely aware of the sensation. The effect was always cumulative; the burden was laid upon him straw by straw.

It began with his being oppressed by the silence of the house. He became more and more acutely conscious of it, until it became like a thing tangible, a prison of solid walls growing around him.

The scratching of his pen at first relieved the tension. He wrote words and erased them again for the sake of that comfortable sound. But presently that comfort was denied him, for it seemed to him that this minute and busy noise was attracting attention to himself. Yes, that was it. He was being watched.

Everton sat quite still, the pen poised an inch above the half-covered sheet of paper. This was become a familiar sensation. He was being watched. And by what? And from what corner of the room?

He forced a tremulous smile to his lips. One moment he called himself ridiculous; the next, he asked himself hopelessly how a man could argue with his nerves. Experience had taught him that the only cure—and that a temporary one—was to go to bed. Yet he sat on, anxious to learn more about himself, to coax his vague imaginings into some definite shape.

Imagination told him that he was being watched, and although he called it imagination he was afraid. That rapid beating against his ribs was his heart, warning him of fear. But he sat rigid, anxious to learn in what part of the room his fancy would place these imaginary "watchers"—for he was conscious of the gaze of more than one pair of eyes being bent upon him.

At first the experiment failed. The rigidity of his pose, the hold he was keeping upon himself, acted as a brake upon his mind. Presently he realized this and relaxed the tension, striving to give his mind that perfect freedom, which might have been demanded by a hypnotist or one experimenting in telepathy.

Almost at once he thought of the door. The eyes of his mind veered round in that direction as the needle of a compass veers to the magnetic north. With these eyes of his imagination he saw the door. It was standing half open, and the aperture was thronged with faces. What kind of faces he could not tell. They were just faces; imagination left it at that. But he was aware that these spies were timid; that they were in some wise as fearful of him as he was of them; that to scatter them he had but to turn his head and gaze at them with the eyes of his body.

The door was at his shoulder. He turned his head suddenly and gave it one swift glance out of the tail of his eye.

However imagination deceived him, it had not played him false about the door. It was standing half open although he could have sworn that he had closed it on entering the room. The aperture was empty. Only darkness, solid as a pillar, filled the space between floor and lintel. But although he saw nothing as he turned his head, he was dimly conscious of something vanishing, a scurrying noiseless and incredibly swift, like the flitting of trout in clear, shallow water.

Everton stood up, stretched himself, and brought his knuckles up to his strained eyes. He told himself that he must go to bed. It was bad enough that he must suffer these nervous attacks; to encourage them was madness.

But as he mounted the stairs he was still conscious of not being alone. Shy, timorous, ready to melt into the shadows of the walls if he turned his head, *they* were following him, whispering noiselessly, linking hands and arms, watching him with the fearful, awed curiosity of—Children.

III

The Vicar had called upon Everton. His name was Parslow, and he was a typical country parson of the poorer sort, a tall, rugged, shabby, worried man in the middle forties, obviously embarrassed by the eternal problem of making ends meet on an inadequate stipend.

Everton received him courteously enough, but with a certain coldness which implied that he had nothing in common with his visitor. Parslow was evidently disappointed because "the new people" were not church-goers nor likely to take much interest in the parish. The two men made half-hearted and vain attempts to find common ground. It was not until he was on the point of leaving that the Vicar mentioned Monica.

"You have, I believe, a little girl?" he said.

"Yes. My small ward."

"Ah! I expect she finds it lonely here. I have a little girl of the same age. She is at present away at school, but she will be home soon for the Easter holidays. I know she would be delighted if your little—er—ward would come down to the Vicarage and play with her sometimes."

The suggestion was not particularly welcome to Everton, and his thanks were perfunctory. This other small girl, although she was a vicar's daughter, might carry the contagion of other modern children and infect Monica with the pertness and slanginess which he so detested. Altogether he was determined to have as little to do with the Vicarage as possible.

Meanwhile the child was becoming to him a study of more and more absorbing interest. The change in her was almost as marked as if she had just returned after having spent a term at school. She astonished and mystified him by using expressions which she could scarcely have learned from any member of the household. It was not the jargon of the smart young people of the day which slipped easily from her lips, but the polite family slang of his own youth. For instance, she remarked one morning that Mead, the gardener, was a whale at pruning vines.

A whale! The expression took Everton back a very long way down the level road of the spent years; took him, indeed, to a nursery in a solid respectable house in a Belgravian square, where he had heard the word used in that same sense for the first time. His sister

Gertrude, aged ten, notorious in those days for picking up loose expressions, announced that she was getting to be a whale at French. Yes, in those days an expert was "whale" or a "don"; not, as he is to-day, a "stout fellow." But who was a "whale" nowadays? It was years since he had heard the term.

"Where did you learn to say that?" he demanded in so strange a tone that Monica stared at him anxiously.

"Isn't it right?" she asked eagerly. She might have been a child at a new school, fearful of not having acquired the fashionable phraseology of the place.

"It is a slang expression," said the purist coldly. "It used to mean a person who was proficient in something. How did you come to hear it?"

She smiled without answering, and her smile was mysterious, even coquettish after a childish fashion. Silence had always been her refuge, but it was no longer a sullen silence. She was changing rapidly, and in a manner to bewilder her guardian. He failed in an effort to cross-examine her, and, later in the day, consulted Miss Gribbin.

"That child," he said, "is reading something that we know nothing about."

"Just at present," said Miss Gribbin, "she is glued to Dickens and Stevenson."

"Then where on earth does she get her expressions?"

"I don't know," the secretary retorted testily, "any more than I know how she learned to play Cat's Cradle."

"What? That game with string? Does she play that?"

"I found her doing something quite complicated and

elaborate the other day. She wouldn't tell me how she learned to do it. I took the trouble to question the servants, but none of them had shown her."

Everton frowned.

"And I know of no book in the library which tells how to perform tricks with string. Do you think she has made a clandestine friendship with any of the village children?"

Miss Gribbin shook her head.

"She is too fastidious for that. Besides, she seldom goes into the village alone."

There, for the time, the discussion ended. Everton, with all the curiosity of the student, watched the child as carefully and closely as he was able without at the same time arousing her suspicions. She was developing fast. He had known that she must develop, but the manner of her doing so amazed and mystified him, and, likely as not, denied some preconceived theory. The untended plant was not only growing but showed signs of pruning. It was as if there were outside influences at work on Monica which could have come neither from him nor from any other member of the household.

Winter was dying hard, and dark days of rain kept Miss Gribbin, Monica and Everton within doors. He lacked no opportunities of keeping the child under observation, and once, on a gloomy afternoon, passing the room which she had named the schoolroom, he paused and listened until he became suddenly aware that his conduct bore an unpleasant resemblance to eavesdropping. The psychologist and the gentleman engaged in a brief struggle in which the gentleman temporarily got the upper hand. Everton approached the door with a heavy step and flung it open.

A. M. BURRAGE

The sensation he received, as he pushed open the
door, was vague but slightly disturbing, and it was by
no means new to him. Several times of late, but generally after dark, he had entered an empty room with
the impression that it had been occupied by others
until the very moment of his crossing the threshold.
His coming disturbed not merely one or two, but a
crowd. He felt rather than heard them scattering,
flying swiftly and silently as shadows to incredible
hiding-places, where they held breath and watched and
waited for him to go. Into the same atmosphere of
tension he now walked, and looked about him as if
expecting to see more than only the child who held
the floor in the middle of the room, or some tell-tale
trace of other children in hiding. Had the room been
furnished he must have looked involuntarily for shoes
protruding from under tables or settees, for ends of
garments unconsciously left exposed.

The long room, however, was empty save for
Monica from wainscot to wainscot and from floor to
ceiling. Fronting him were the long high windows
starred by fine rain. With her back to the white filtered
light Monica faced him, looking up to him as he entered. He was just in time to see a smile fading from
her lips. He also saw by a slight convulsive movement
of her shoulders that she was hiding something from
him in the hands clasped behind her back.

"Hullo," he said, with a kind of forced geniality,
"what are you up to?"

She said: "Nothing," but not as sullenly as she
would once have said it.

"Come," said Everton, "that is impossible. You
were talking to yourself, Monica. You should not do

that. It is an idle and very, very foolish habit. You will go mad if you continue to do that."

She let her head droop a little.

"I wasn't talking to myself," she said in a low, half playful but very deliberate tone.

"That's nonsense. I heard you."

"I wasn't talking to myself."

"But you must have been. There is nobody else here."

"There isn't—now."

"What do you mean? Now?"

"They've gone. You frightened them, I expect."

"What do you mean?" he repeated, advancing a step or two towards her. "And whom do you call 'they'?"

Next moment he was angry with himself. His tone was so heavy and serious and the child was half laughing at him. It was as if she were triumphant at having inveigled him into taking a serious part in her own game of make-believe.

"You wouldn't understand," she said.

"I understand this—that you are wasting your time and being a very silly little girl. What's that you're hiding behind your back?"

She held out her right hand at once, unclenched her fingers and disclosed a thimble. He looked at it and then into her face.

"Why did you hide that from me?" he asked. "There was no need."

She gave him a faint secretive smile—that new smile of hers—before replying.

"We were playing with it. I didn't want you to know."

"*You* were playing with it, you mean. And why didn't you want me to know?"

"About them. Because I thought you wouldn't understand. You *don't* understand."

He saw that it was useless to affect anger or show impatience. He spoke to her gently, even with an attempt at displaying sympathy.

"Who are 'they'?" he asked.

"They're just them. Other girls."

"I see. And they come and play with you, do they? And they run away whenever I'm about, because they don't like me. Is that it?"

She shook her head.

"It isn't that they don't like you. I think they like everybody. But they're so shy. They were shy of me for a long, long time. I know they were there, but it was weeks and weeks before they'd come and play with me. It was weeks before I even saw them."

"Yes? Well, what are they like?"

"Oh, they're just girls. And they're awfully, awfully nice. Some are a bit older than me and some are a bit younger. And they don't dress like other girls you see to-day. They're in white with longer skirts and they wear sashes."

Everton inclined his head gravely. "She got that out of the illustrations of books in the library," he reflected.

"You don't happen to know their names, I suppose?" he asked, hoping that no quizzical note in his voice rang through the casual but sincere tone which he intended.

"Oh, yes. There's Mary Hewitt—I think I love her best of all—and Elsie Power and—"

"How many of them altogether?"

"Seven. It's just a nice number. And this is the schoolroom where we play games. I love games. I wish I'd learned to play games before."

"And you've been playing with the thimble?"

"Yes. Hunt-the-thimble they call it. One of us hides it, and then the rest of us try to find it, and the one who finds it hides it again."

"You mean you hide it yourself, and then go and find it."

The smile left her face at once, and the look in her eyes warned him that she was done with confidences.

"Ah!" she exclaimed. "You don't understand after all. I somehow knew you wouldn't."

Everton, however, thought he did. His face wore a sudden smile of relief.

"Well, never mind," he said. "But I shouldn't play too much if I were you."

With that he left her. But curiosity tempted him, not in vain, to linger and listen for a moment on the other side of the door which he had closed behind him. He heard Monica whisper:

"Mary! Elsie! Come on. It's all right. He's gone now."

At an answering whisper, very unlike Monica's, he started violently and then found himself grinning at his own discomfiture. It was natural that Monica, playing many parts, should try to change her voice with every character. He went downstairs sunk in a brown study which brought him to certain interesting conclusions. A little later he communicated these to Miss Gribbin.

"I've discovered the cause of the change in Monica. She's invented for herself some imaginary friends—other little girls, of course."

Miss Gribbin started slightly and looked up from the newspaper which she had been reading.

"Really?" she exclaimed. "Isn't that rather an unhealthy sign?"

"No, I should say not. Having imaginary friends is quite a common symptom of childhood, especially among young girls. I remember my sister used to have one, and was very angry when none of the rest of us would take the matter seriously. In Monica's case I should say it was perfectly normal—normal, but interesting. She must have inherited an imagination from that father of hers, with the result that she has seven imaginary friends, all properly named, if you please. You see, being lonely, and having no friends of her own age, she would naturally invent more than one 'friend.' They are all nicely and primly dressed, I must tell you, out of Victorian books which she has found in the library."

"It can't be healthy," said Miss Gribbin, pursing her lips. "And I can't understand how she has learned certain expressions and a certain style of talking and games—"

"All out of books. And pretends to herself that 'they' have taught her. But the most interesting part of the affair is this: it's given me my first practical experience of telepathy, of the existence of which I have hitherto been rather sceptical. Since Monica invented this new game, and before I was aware that she had done so, I have had at different times distinct impressions of there being a lot of little girls about the house."

Miss Gribbin started and stared. Her lips parted as if she were about to speak, but it was as if she had

changed her mind while framing the first word she had
been about to utter.

"Monica," he continued smiling, "invented these
'friends,' and has been making me telepathically aware
of them, too. I have lately been most concerned about
the state of my nerves."

Miss Gribbin jumped up as if in anger, but her
brow was smooth and her mouth dropped at the cor-
ners.

"Mr. Everton," she said, "I wish you had not told
me all this." Her lips worked. "You see," she added
unsteadily, "I don't believe in telepathy."

IV

Easter, which fell early that year, brought little
Gladys Parslow home for the holidays to the Vicarage.
The event was shortly afterwards signalized by a note
from the Vicar to Everton, inviting him to send Monica down to have tea and play games with his little
daughter on the following Wednesday.

The invitation was an annoyance and an embarrassment to Everton. Here was the disturbing factor, the
outside influence, which might possibly thwart his experiment in the upbringing of Monica. He was free,
of course, simply to decline the invitation so coldly and
briefly as to make sure that it would not be repeated;
but the man was not strong enough to stand on his own
feet impervious to the winds of criticism. He was sensitive and had little wish to seem churlish, still less to
appear ridiculous. Taking the line of least resistance he
began to reason that one child, herself no older than
Monica, and in the atmosphere of her own home, could

make but little impression. It ended in his allowing
Monica to go.

Monica herself seemed pleased at the prospect of
going but expressed her pleasure in a discreet, restrained, grown-up way. Miss Gribbin accompanied
her as far as the Vicarage doorstep, arriving with her
punctually at half-past three on a sullen and muggy
afternoon, and handed her over to the woman-of-all-
work who answered the summons at the door.

Miss Gribbin reported to Everton on her return.
An idea which she conceived to be humorous had possession of her mind, and in talking to Everton she uttered one of her infrequent laughs.

"I only left her at the door," she said, "so I didn't
see her meet the other little girl. I wish I'd stayed to
see that. It must have been funny."

She irritated Everton by speaking exactly as if Monica were a captive animal which had just been shown,
for the first time in its life, another of its own kind.
The analogy thus conveyed to Everton was close
enough to make him wince. He felt something like a
twinge of conscience, and it may have been then that he
asked himself for the first time if he were being fair to
Monica.

It had never once occurred to him to ask himself if
she were happy. The truth was that he understood
children so little as to suppose that physical cruelty was
the one kind of cruelty from which they were capable
of suffering. Had he ever before troubled to ask himself if Monica were happy, he had probably given the
question a curt dismissal with the thought that she had
no right to be otherwise. He had given her a good
home, even luxuries, together with every opportunity

to develop her mind. For companions she had himself,
Miss Gribbin, and, to a limited extent, the servants.

Ah, but that picture, conjured up by Miss Gribbin's
words with their accompaniment of unreasonable
laughter! The little creature meeting for the first time
another little creature of its own kind and looking bewildered, knowing neither what to do nor what to say.
There was pathos in that—uncomfortable pathos for
Everton. Those imaginary friends—did they really
mean that Monica had needs of which he knew nothing, of which he had never troubled to learn?

He was not an unkind man, and it hurt him to suspect that he might have committed an unkindness. The
modern children whose behavior and manners he disliked, were perhaps only obeying some inexorable law
of evolution. Suppose in keeping Monica from their
companionship he were actually flying in the face of
Nature? Suppose, after all, if Monica were to be natural, she must go unhindered on the tide of her gen-
eration?

He compromised with himself, pacing the little
study. He would watch Monica much more closely,
question her when he had the chance. Then, if he
found she was not happy, and really needed the companionship of other children, he would see what could
be done.

But when Monica returned home from the Vicarage
it was quite plain that she had not enjoyed herself. She
was subdued, and said very little about her experience.
Quite obviously the two little girls had not made very
good friends. Questioned, Monica confessed that she
did not like Gladys—much. She said this very thoughtfully with a little pause before the adverb.

"Why don't you like her?" Everton demanded bluntly.

"I don't know. She's so funny. Not like other girls."

"And what do you know about other girls?" he demanded, faintly amused.

"Well, she's not a bit like—"

Monica paused suddenly and lowered her gaze.

"Not like your 'friends,' you mean?" Everton asked.

She gave him a quick, penetrating little glance and then lowered her gaze once more.

"No," she said, "not a bit."

She wouldn't be, of course. Everton teased the child with no more questions for the time being, and let her go. She ran off at once to the great empty room, there to seek that uncanny companionship which had come to suffice her.

For the moment Everton was satisfied. Monica was perfectly happy as she was, and had no need of Gladys or, probably, any other child friends. His experiment with her was shaping successfully. She had invented her own young friends, and had gone off eagerly to play with the creations of her own fancy.

This seemed very well at first. Everton reflected that it was just what he would have wished, until he realized suddenly with a little shock of discomfort that it was not normal and it was not healthy.

V

Although Monica plainly had no great desire to see any more of Gladys Parslow, common civility made it necessary for the Vicar's little daughter to be asked to pay a return visit. Most likely Gladys Parslow was as unwilling to come as was Monica to entertain her. Stern discipline, however, presented her at the appointed time on an afternoon pre-arranged by correspondence, when Monica received her coldly and with dignity, tempered by a sort of grown-up graciousness.

Monica bore her guest away to the big empty room, and that was the last of Gladys Parslow seen of Everton or Miss Gribbin that afternoon. Monica appeared alone when the gong sounded for tea, and announced in a subdued tone that Gladys had already gone home.

"Did you quarrel with her?" Miss Gribbin asked quickly.

"No-o."

"Then why has she gone like this?"

"She was stupid," said Monica, simply. "That's all."

"Perhaps it was you who was stupid. Why did she go?"

"She got frightened."

"Frightened!"

"She didn't like my friends."

Miss Gribbin exchanged glances with Everton.

"She didn't like a silly little girl who talks to herself and imagines things. No wonder she was frightened."

"She didn't think they were real at first, and laughed at me," said Monica, sitting down.

"Naturally!"

"And then when she saw them—"

Miss Gribbin and Everton interrupted her simultaneously, repeating in unison and with well-matched astonishment, her two last words.

"And when she saw them," Monica continued, unperturbed, "she didn't like it. I think she was frightened. Anyhow, she said she wouldn't stay and went straight off home. I think she's a stupid girl. We all had a good laugh about her after she was gone."

She spoke in her ordinary matter-of-fact tones, and if she were secretly pleased at the state of perturbation into which her last words had obviously thrown Miss Gribbin she gave no sign of it. Miss Gribbin immediately exhibited outward signs of anger.

"You are a very naughty child to tell such untruths. You know perfectly well that Gladys couldn't have *seen* your 'friends.' You have simply frightened her by pretending to talk to people who weren't there, and it will serve you right if she never comes to play with you again."

"She won't," said Monica. "And she *did* see them, Miss Gribbin."

"How do you know?" Everton asked.

"By her face. And she spoke to them too, when she ran to the door. They were very shy at first because Gladys was there. They wouldn't come for a long time, but I begged them, and at last they did."

Everton checked another outburst from Miss Gribbin with a look. He wanted to learn more, and to that end he applied some show of patience and gentleness.

"Where did they come from?" he asked. "From outside the door?"

"Oh, no. From where they always come."

"And where's that?"

"I don't know. They don't seem to know themselves. It's always from some direction where I'm not looking. Isn't it strange?"

"Very! And do they disappear in the same way?"

Monica frowned very seriously and thoughtfully.

"It's so quick you can't tell where they go. When you or Miss Gribbin come in—"

"They always fly on our approach, of course. But why?"

"Because they're dreadfully, dreadfully shy. But not so shy as they were. Perhaps soon they'll get used to you and not mind at all."

"That's a comforting thought!" said Everton with a dry laugh.

When Monica had taken her tea and departed, Everton turned to his secretary.

"You are wrong to blame the child. These creatures of her fancy are perfectly real to her. Her powers of suggestion have been strong enough to force them to some extent on me. The little Parslow girl, being younger and more receptive, actually *sees* them. It is a clear case of telepathy and auto-suggestion. I have never studied such matters, but I should say that these instances are of some scientific interest."

Miss Gribbin's lips tightened and he saw her shiver slightly.

"Mr. Parslow will be angry," was all she said.

"I really cannot help that. Perhaps it is all for the best. If Monica does not like his little daughter they had better not be brought together again."

For all that, Everton was a little embarrassed when on the following morning he met the Vicar out walking. If the Reverend Mr. Parslow knew that his little daughter had left the house so unceremoniously on the preceding day, he would either wish to make an apology, or perhaps require one, according to his view of the situation. Everton did not wish to deal in apologies one way or the other, he did not care to discuss the vagaries of children, and altogether he wanted to have as little to do with Mr. Parslow as was conveniently possible. He would have passed with a brief acknowledgement of the Vicar's existence, but, as he had feared, the Vicar stopped him.

"I had been meaning to come and see you," said the Reverend Mr. Parslow.

Everton halted and sighed inaudibly, thinking that perhaps this casual meeting out of doors might after all have saved him something.

"Yes?" he said.

"I will walk in your direction if I may." The Vicar eyed him anxiously. "There is something you must certainly be told. I don't know if you guess, or if you already know. If not, I don't know how you will take it. I really don't."

"Really?" he asked. "Is it something serious?"

"I think so, Mr. Everton. You are aware, of course, that my little girl left your house yesterday afternoon with some lack of ceremony."

"Yes, Monica told us she had gone. If they could not agree it was surely the best thing she could have done, although it may sound inhospitable of me to say it. Excuse me, Mr. Parslow, but I hope you are not trying to embroil me in a quarrel between children?"

The Vicar stared in his turn.

"I am not," he said, "and I am unaware that there was any quarrel. I was going to ask you to forgive Gladys. There was some excuse for her lack of ceremony. She was badly frightened, poor child."

"Then it is my turn to express regret. I had Monica's version of what happened. Monica has been left a great deal to her own resources, and, having no playmates of her own age, she seems to have invented some."

"Ah!" said the Reverend Mr. Parslow, drawing a deep breath.

"Unfortunately," Everton continued, "Monica has an uncomfortable gift for impressing her fancies on other people. I have often thought I felt the presence of children about the house, and so, I am almost sure, has Miss Gribbin. I am afraid that when your little girl came to play with her yesterday afternoon, Monica scared her by introducing her invisible 'friends' and by talking to imaginary and therefore invisible little girls."

The Vicar laid a hand on Everton's arm.

"There is something more in it than that. Gladys is not an imaginative child; she is, indeed, a practical little person. I have never yet known her to tell me a lie. What would you say, Mr. Everton, if I were to tell you that Gladys positively asserts that she *saw* those other children?"

Something like a cold draught went through Everton. An ugly suspicion, vague and almost shapeless, began to move in dim recesses of his mind. He tried to shake himself free of it, to smile and to speak lightly.

"I shouldn't be in the least surprised. Nobody knows the limits of telepathy and auto-suggestion. If I can feel the presence of children whom Monica has created out of her own imagination, why shouldn't your daughter, who is probably more receptive and impressionable than I am, be able to see them?"

The Reverend Mr. Parslow shook his head.

"Do you really mean that?" he asked. "Doesn't it seem to you a little far-fetched?"

"Everything we don't understand must seem far-fetched. If one had dared to talk of wireless thirty years ago—"

"Mr. Everton, do you know that your house was once a girls' school?"

Once more Everton experienced that vague feeling of discomfiture.

"I didn't know," he said, still indifferently.

"My aunt, whom I never saw, was there. Indeed she died there. There were seven who died. Diphtheria broke out there many years ago. It ruined the school which was shortly afterwards closed. Did you know that, Mr. Everton? My aunt's name was Mary Hewitt—"

"Good God!" Everton cried out sharply. "Good God!"

"Ah!" said Parslow. "Now do you begin to see?"

Everton, suddenly a little giddy, passed a hand across his forehead.

"That is—one of the names Monica told me," he faltered. "How could she know?"

"How indeed? Mary Hewitt's great friend was Elsie Power. They died within a few hours of each other."

"That name too . . . she told me . . . and there were seven. How could she have known? Even the people around here wouldn't have remembered names after all these years."

"Gladys knew them. But that was only partly why she was afraid. Yet I think she was more awed than afraid, because she knew instinctively that the children who came to play with little Monica, although they were not of this world, were good children, blessed children."

"What are you telling me?" Everton burst out.

"Don't be afraid, Mr. Everton. You are not afraid, are you? If those whom we call dead still remain close to us, what more natural than these children should come back to play with a lonely little girl who lacked human playmates? It may seem inconceivable, but how else explain it? How could little Monica have invented those two names? How could she have learned that seven little girls once died in your house? Only the very old people about here remember it, and even they could not tell you how many died or the name of any one of the little victims. Haven't you noticed a change in your ward since first she began to—imagine them, as you thought?"

Everton nodded heavily.

"Yes," he said, almost unwittingly, "she learned all sorts of tricks of speech, childish gestures she never had before, and games. . . . I couldn't understand. Mr. Parslow, what in God's name am I to do?"

The Reverend Mr. Parslow still kept a hand on Everton's arm.

"If I were you I should send her off to school. It may not be very good for her."

"Not good for her! But the children, you say—"

"Children? I might have said angels. *They* will never harm her. But Monica is developing a gift of seeing and conversing with—with beings that are invisible and inaudible to others. It is not a gift to be encouraged. She may in time see and converse with others—wretched souls who are not God's children. She may lose the faculty if she mixes with others of her age. Out of her need, I am sure, these came to her."

"I must think," said Everton.

He walked on dazedly. In a moment or two the

whole aspect of life had changed, had grown clearer, as if he had been blind from birth and was now given the first glimmerings of light. He looked forward no longer into the face of a blank and featureless wall, but through a curtain beyond which life manifested itself vaguely but at least perceptibly. His footfalls on the ground beat out the words. "There is no death. There is no death."

VI

That evening after dinner he sent for Monica and spoke to her in an unaccustomed way. He was strangely shy of her, and his hand, which he rested on one of her slim shoulders, lay there awkwardly.

"Do you know what I'm going to do with you, young woman?" he said. "I'm going to pack you off to school."

"O-oh!" she stared at him, half smiling. "Are you really?"

"Do you want to go?"

She considered the matter, frowning and staring at the tips of her fingers.

"I don't know. I don't want to leave *them*."

"Who?" he asked.

"Oh, you know!" she said, and turned her head half shyly.

"What? Your—friends, Monica?"

"Yes."

"Wouldn't you like other playmates?"

"I don't know. I love *them*, you see. But they said —they said I ought to go to school if you ever sent me. They might be angry with me if I was to ask you to let me stay. They wanted me to play with other girls who aren't—what aren't like they are. Because you know, they are *different* from children that everybody can see. And Mary told me not to—not to encourage anybody else who was different, like them."

Everton drew a deep breath.

"We'll have a talk tomorrow about finding a school for you, Monica," he said. "Run off to bed, now. Good-night, my dear."

He hesitated, then touched her forehead with his lips. She ran from him, nearly as shy as Everton himself, tossing back her long hair, but from the door she gave him the strangest little brimming glance, and there was that in her eyes which he had never seen before.

Late that night Everton entered the great empty room which Monica had named the schoolroom. A flag of moonlight from the window lay across the floor, and it was empty to the gaze. But the deep shadows hid little shy presences of which some unnamed and undeveloped sense in the man was acutely aware.

"Children!" he whispered. "Children!"

He closed his eyes and stretched out his hands. Still they were shy and held aloof, but he fancied that they came a little nearer.

"Don't be afraid," he whispered. "I'm only a very lonely man. Be near me after Monica is gone."

He paused, waiting. Then as he turned away he was aware of little caressing hands upon his arm. He looked around at once, but the time had not yet come for him to see. He saw only the barred window, the shadows on either wall and the flag of moonlight.

HUGH PENTECOST

My Dear Uncle Sherlock

*"I believe Sherlock Holmes is considered to be some-
thing of a classic these days," Esther Trimble said.
"Classic fol-de-rol!" Hector said. "Cluttering his mind
with sensational nonsense."*

Joey Trimble, aged twelve, looking very much over-
scrubbed and overdressed for a weekday morning, sat
meekly in his place at the breakfast table listening to
his father's tirade. Hector Trimble, the local druggist,
was speaking to his wife, but every word was meant for
Joey.

"If it were not," Hector said in his prim way, "for
Joey's association with your brother George, I would
not be losing half a day's business at the store, and a
twelve-year-old boy would not find himself in the incredible position of being a witness in a murder case."

"I don't know what George has to do with the murder of old Mrs. Leggett," Esther Trimble said mildly. "Have some more coffee, Father?"

"I do not wish any more coffee," Hector said. "I merely wish to say what is on my mind, and without interruption, *please!* If it were not for Uncle George, Joey would not have been interesting himself in trying to make friends with a vicious dog that would make friends with no one. If it were not for this absurd attempt to make friends with a vicious dog, Joey would not have discovered the dog dead. If he had not discovered the dog dead, he would not have gone for Trooper Gilligan, and he would not have gone into the house with Trooper Gilligan and found old Mrs. Leggett with her throat cut."

"The dog's throat was cut too, Father," Joey said, in an effort to keep the facts straight.

"That is immaterial," Hector said. He turned on his son. "How, may I ask, do you spend these winter afternoons when it is too stormy for you to be wasting your time hunting, or fishing through holes in the ice, or prowling through the woods with George Crowder? Do you take the opportunity to study your mathematics or your history, in both of which you are woefully deficient? You do not! I happen to know exactly what you are doing."

"I—I'm improving my mind," Joey said hesitantly.

Hector snorted. "He's improving his mind! Do you know how he does that, my dear Esther? He goes to your brother George's shack, and there your brother George, who hasn't done a stroke of work in fifteen years, reads aloud to him."

"I don't see any harm in that, Father," Esther Trimble said. "I'd much rather he'd absorb a little literature than watch some of the programs we get on television."

"Literature!" Hector rose, cold, dignified, and crossed to the sideboard. He opened a drawer and took out two objects. One was an old fashioned deerstalker cap. The other was a magnifying glass. "Literature!" Hector repeated. "Lurid nonsense! *The Memoirs of Sherlock Holmes!* Running about the streets in this nonsensical hat! Peering through this glass at footprints in the snow!"

"I believe Sherlock Holmes is considered to be something of a classic these days," Esther Trimble said.

"Classic fol-de-rol!" Hector said. "Cluttering his mind with sensational nonsense. I tell you, Esther—"

"You and Joey will be late, Father," Esther said calmly. "You were called for the Grand Jury hearing at ten o'clock."

"Very well," Hector said. "But just remember, I haven't finished. Tonight I shall—"

"And don't forget to wear your rubbers, Father," Esther Trimble said.

The steam pipes in the jury room at the Lakeview Town Hall pounded steadily like some sort of mechanical pulse. The room was hot and overcrowded, and the air was stale. Hector Trimble and his son Joey sat in the front row of chairs reserved for witnesses. Beside them were old Dave Taylor, custodian of the grammar school and janitor of the Presbyterian Church, who had also taken care of the grounds and the furnace of old Mrs. Leggett, and Trooper Gilligan, who was the resident representative of the State Police in Lakeview.

Across the room to one side sat Bill Leggett and his

wife, Joan. Bill Leggett rested his elbows on the arms of his chair, and his hands were raised to cover his haggard face. Joan Leggett sat beside him, her hand on his arm, her head held high and proud. She was pretty darned beautiful, Joey told himself—old, of course, but just about the most beautiful woman he'd ever seen. Joey had remarked about it once to his Uncle George who had nodded sagely.

"It is remarkable, Joey," Uncle George had said. "Twenty-five years old and hardly faded a drop!"

Joey knew almost everyone on the jury, especially Red Egan, the foreman. Red used to go hunting in season with Joey and Uncle George and Uncle George's setter, Timmy. Next to Uncle George, Red Egan was about the best man in the woods Joey had ever seen. Joey knew that if some day he could be as good as Red Egan he'd be quite happy. Nobody, of course, could be as good as Uncle George.

Young Mr. Patrick Aloysius Molloy, the County Prosecutor, rumpled his thick hair as he glanced at a sheaf of papers in his hand. Finally he turned to the jury. Joey was aware of a happy sigh sweeping over the packed courtroom behind him.

"Gentlemen of the jury," Pat Molloy began. "It is my unhappy task this morning to present some gruesome facts to you to determine whether a just indictment can be handed down against William Leggett for the brutal slaying of his great aunt, Mrs. Lydia Leggett."

"And her dog!" Joey hadn't intended to speak. The words had just popped out of him. There was a snicker behind him, and Hector Trimble blushed scarlet. His hand closed firmly on his son's wrist.

Mr. Patrick Aloysius Molloy knew how to play his

cards. He turned the moment to his own advantage. He smiled benignly at Joey. "Our young friend is quite correct. '*And* her dog!' If anything were needed to show the cold-blooded purposefulness of the murderer, the killing of Mrs. Leggett's dog is all that would be needed. The killing of that dog, gentlemen, shows that this brutal crime was premeditated, carefully planned, calculated down to the last detail.

"Through the testimony of certain witnesses, gentlemen of the jury, I propose to establish certain facts, some of them already known to you." Molloy glanced once more at his papers. "I propose to establish the fact that Mrs. Lydia Leggett, aged seventy-seven, had been a widow for twenty-four years. When Mrs. Leggett's husband died, she became something of a recluse, even though she lived on the main street of our town. I have been unable to find a single person in Lakeview who has ever seen Mrs. Leggett outside her house during the past twenty years, or anyone who has ever been inside that house. Her supplies, her food and other needs, have been delivered to the back porch of her house over all this time, where the deliverer always found the cash waiting for him.

"Notice that fact, gentlemen—the cash! I propose to show that Mrs. Leggett had no known bank account in this town or anywhere else. She always paid in cash! Even her annual donation of five thousand dollars to the local charity drive was paid in cash. I guess every resident of this community has long been aware of the probability that Mrs. Leggett had a large sum of cash in her possession at all times.

"Imprudent as such behavior may seem, Mrs. Leggett was not entirely without thought of her own protection. Over the years she has had a series of dogs—three, I believe—famous for their qualities as watchdogs. The most recent—a German police dog named Shep—was, as you know, something of a marvel to the village. It never went outside the picket fence that surrounds Mrs. Leggett's house. It never barked indiscriminately. But let anyone so much as put a hand on the fence gate and Shep would announce the fact with sharp, vicious barking. If anyone had the temerity to open the gate and step inside, that person was liable to savage attack. Mr. Dave Taylor, who did odd jobs for Mrs. Leggett, was the only person in Lakeview whom Shep would tolerate. Mr. Taylor will testify to this—and to the really dangerous and extraordinary qualities as a watchdog that Shep possessed.

"Another witness to the characteristics of Shep will be Trooper Gilligan, who, is all of you know, lives in the house adjoining Mrs. Leggett's. And young Master Joey Trimble, who was good enough to remind us of Shep—" Molloy smiled warmly at Joey, "and who has a reputation for being an extremely good handler of hunting dogs despite his meager years, will testify that he had tried to make friends with Shep, but to no avail.

"Now, gentlemen, this same Master Joey Trimble is in the habit of rising early. It stormed the night before last, as you may recall, but the next morning was bright and clear. Young Master Trimble, ambling along Main Street at about six A.M., paused outside the picket fence surrounding Mrs. Leggett's house, his mind no doubt involved with the project of making friends with Shep. But suddenly he became aware he would never have the opportunity to achieve his goal, for he saw Shep lying on the back porch of the house in a welter of blood. Young Master Trimble saw at a glance that the dog was dead.

"Using his head admirably, Young Master Trimble ran to Trooper Gilligan's house and summoned aid. He and Trooper Gilligan proceeded to Mrs. Leggett's back porch where they saw the dog had been dead for some time. The body was frozen stiff. They could see the gaping wound where the faithful animal's throat had been cut.

"They then entered the Leggett house. The place, Trooper Gilligan will testify, looked as if it had been struck by a cyclone—furniture overturned, drawers ripped out and emptied, upholstery slashed, and dishes scattered. And at the foot of the stairs lay old Mrs. Leggett. Like the dog, her throat had been cut."

Molloy waited for this to sink in.

"Bear in mind, gentlemen, no one could have entered that house without a loud and fierce warning from Shep. Bear in mind that Trooper Gilligan was at home next door the entire evening and night, and will swear there was no such outcry. We know why. The dog was destroyed to keep it quiet. Only one person could have entered that yard without Shep's giving the alarm—old Dave Taylor." Molloy glanced at the witness sitting next to Hector. "Shep would have allowed Dave to enter without protest. It must become immediately obvious that the one person who had safe access to the house, Dave Taylor, is cleared by this very fact. It would not have been necessary for him to kill the dog. Shep would have let him pass without protest.

"Gentlemen, the motive for this brutal crime is obvious. Money—the considerable sum in cash known to be secreted by Mrs. Leggett. It will be my unpleasant duty, gentlemen, to show that William Leggett, great nephew of the deceased, was in desperate need of funds. William Leggett, as we all know, has no permanent employment. It is no secret that as recently as ten days ago his car was repossessed by the finance company. It is no secret that he had attempted to borrow from his great aunt, but without success. I will show that he made a public attempt—over the phone in the bar at the Red Lion—early on the evening of the murder, and was turned down.

"I will show, through witnesses, that he made threats against his aunt in public after that refusal. I will show, through witnesses, that he was seen loitering outside the fence of Mrs. Leggett's house later that evening. William Leggett says he was trying to get up the nerve to ask his aunt for money face to face, but that he lost his nerve, and went home. It will be my task to cast more than reasonable doubt on that story, gentlemen—to convince you, as I am convinced, that William Leggett waited until his great aunt had let her dog, Shep, out for the last time that night, that he crept up on the dog and cut its throat, that he then entered the house and did away with his aunt in the same manner, and then proceeded—for what must have been hours—to search for the money. And now, gentlemen, if there are no questions I shall call my first witness."

"I got a question, Pat," Red Egan said from the jury box. "Does William Leggett have legal counsel for this here hearing?"

"Mr. Leggett has waived his right to counsel," Molloy said. "He is without funds to engage counsel. Of course, if he is indicted and brought to trial, the court will appoint an attorney for his defense."

A familiar voice, clear and dry, made Joey Trimble jerk his head around. It came from the back of the courtroom. Old George Crowder stood there, tall and angular. His clear blue eyes were frosty-cold. "I would be happy to represent William Leggett—funds or no funds," Uncle George said. "Shouldn't take over five minutes, Mr. Molloy, to show that you're wasting the town's money, and worse than that, you're wasting the town's time. Money you can dig up somewhere, but you can never recover time."

Hector Trimble lowered his head. His shiftless brother-in-law was about to make fools of them. True, George Crowder had been a brilliant lawyer years ago —he'd been County Prosecutor like Molloy; but he'd sent a man to the electric chair for murder—a man who later had been proved innocent—and he'd dropped his practice, moved into the woods, and become a shiftless ne'er-do-well and the particular burden of Hector's life.

Patrick Aloysius Molloy regarded Uncle George without pleasure. He had had a few encounters with the old man, and none of them had turned out happily for Molloy. He turned, scowling, to the young Leggetts. "Do you wish to avail yourselves of Mr. Crowder's offer?"

Bill Leggett nodded. Joan Leggett, her head still high, spoke in a clear voice. "We'd be proud and grateful."

There was a murmur of excitement as Uncle George made his way down the aisle. Uncle George, they knew, was a "character"—you could expect something entertaining from him.

Uncle George paused by Joey's chair and put his strong bony hand on Joey's shoulder. He winked down at his nephew. "The facts seem rather obvious, don't they, my dear Watson?"

Joey blinked. "N-no, sir," he said.

"Tut, tut, Watson, where are your powers of observation? I think we shall have to give the prosecutor a few hints."

"This is not a place for fancy games, Mr. Crowder," Molloy said angrily.

"Quite so," Uncle George said. "My apologies. But my nephew and I have recently been reading the works of Doctor A. Conan Doyle and we kind of got into the habit of talking to each other that way."

"George!" Hector whispered, shocked. Enough was enough—this was a court of law!

"My client isn't the murderer, however, Mr. Molloy. Just from hearing the facts I can tell you quite a few things about the real murderer." Again Uncle George glanced at Joey, his eyes twinkling. "The murderer, my dear Molloy, is about five feet seven inches tall, gray-haired, left-handed, suffering from arthritis, carries a clasp knife with a badly nicked blade, chews tobacco, is a teetotaler, suffers from astigmatism which he corrects with glasses when he reads, and voted for Adlai Stevenson in the last Presidential election." Uncle George beamed at the gaping Molloy. "My client fits absolutely none of those descriptive facts, Mr. Prosecutor, and so I demand his release. However, with the facts I've given you, you should have very little trouble putting your hands on the guilty party."

Molloy banged his fist on the railing in front of the jury box. "What kind of outrageous nonsense are you trying to hand us?" he shouted.

"Not nonsense," Uncle George said calmly. "Accurate and factual."

Old Dave Taylor, sitting next to Hector Trimble, chuckled. "Funny thing, Mr. Crowder," he said, "but that description of yours fits me to a T. But everyone knows it wasn't me, because I was the one person who wouldn't have had to kill the dog. Shep wouldn't have done no barking at me."

The twinkle had gone out of Uncle George's eyes and they were colder now than the winter sky outside the courtroom windows. "On the contrary, Dave, you're the one person, more than any other, *who had to kill the dog*. If Mrs. Leggett was found murdered and her house ransacked and the dog alive—and Trooper Gilligan right next door to testify that the dog never barked—you'd have been chucked in jail before you could say 'Dave Taylor.' You *had* to kill the dog, Dave."

Old Dave Taylor's face seemed suddenly to go out of focus. "But I tell you—"

"Don't tell me anything, Dave," Uncle George said. "I don't know about you, Mr. Molloy, but Red Egan, the honorable foreman of this jury, knows something about dogs. How much chance would a man have: Red, sneaking up over that crisp, dry snow and grabbing that dog and cutting its throat without the dog setting up a holler long before the murderer could get close enough to lay a hand on Shep?"

Red Egan shook his head slowly, a broad grin spreading over his face. Uncle George turned back to Molloy.

"If the dog had been shot or poisoned—well, we might have an argument, Molloy. But someone got close enough to Shep to take hold of the dog and put a knife to its throat without Shep's letting out a single yip! There wasn't a living soul but Dave who could do that."

The courtroom was suddenly noisy with excitement. Old Dave Taylor was shouting at the top of his lungs: "I couldn't stand it no longer. Her with all that money, and never a Christmas present, never an extra dime, never nothing. In twenty-four long years—"

Trooper Gilligan took old Dave by the arm. "Come on, Dave."

Bill Leggett was pounding Uncle George's back and Joan Leggett's eyes were bright as two stars.

"You old fraud!" Bill cried. "Most of it I admit you could see if you knew where to look. But how did you know about the knife—and how about him voting for Stevenson?"

"Been fishing with him," Uncle George said. "Seen him clean a catch with that knife. And being a Democrat myself, I happen to know he's one of only a dozen registered Democrats in the whole town of Lakeview." Uncle George looked down at Joey. "I fear when these little problems have been solved and explained they seem altogether too elementary, my dear Watson."

Joey hugged himself with delight. "Amazing, my dear Uncle Sherlock," he said. "Amazing!"

JEROME BIXBY

It's a Good Life

*Bill Soames vanished down the road in a cloud of dust,
his thin, terrified wail drifting back across the summerlike heat.*

Aunt Amy was out on the front porch, rocking back
and forth in the highbacked chair and fanning herself,
when Bill Soames rode his bicycle up the road and
stopped in front of the house.

Perspiring under the afternoon "sun," Bill lifted the
box of groceries out of the big basket over the front
wheel of the bike, and came up the front walk.

Little Anthony was sitting on the lawn, playing with
a rat. He had caught the rat down in the basement—he
had made it think that it smelled cheese, the most rich-
smelling and crumbly-delicious cheese a rat had ever
thought it smelled, and it had come out of its hole,
and now Anthony had hold of it with his mind and
was making it do tricks.

When the rat saw Bill Soames coming, it tried to run,

but Anthony thought at it, and it turned a flip-flop on the grass, and lay trembling, its eyes gleaming in small black terror.

Bill Soames hurried past Anthony and reached the front steps, mumbling. He always mumbled when he came to the Fremont house, or passed by it, or even thought of it. Everybody did. They thought about silly things, things that didn't mean very much, like two-and-two-is-four-and-twice-is-eight and so on; they tried to jumble up their thoughts and keep them skipping back and forth, so Anthony couldn't read their minds. The mumbling helped. Because if Anthony got anything strong out of your thoughts, he might take a notion to do something about it—like curing your wife's sick headaches or your kid's mumps, or getting your old milk cow back on schedule, or fixing the privy. And while Anthony mightn't actually mean any harm, he couldn't be expected to have much notion of what was the right thing to do in such cases.

That was if he liked you. He might try to help you, in his way. And that could be pretty horrible.

If he didn't like you . . . well, that could be worse.

Bill Soames set the box of groceries on the porch railing, and stopped his mumbling long enough to say, "Everythin' you wanted, Miss Amy."

"Oh, fine, William," Amy Fremont said lightly. "My, ain't it terrible hot today?"

Bill Soames almost cringed. His eyes pleaded with her. He shook his head violently *no,* and then interrupted his mumbling again, though obviously he didn't want to: "Oh, don't say that, Miss Amy . . . it's fine, just fine. A real *good* day!"

Amy Fremont got up from the rocking chair, and came across the porch. She was a tall woman, thin, a smiling vacancy in her eyes. About a year ago, Anthony had gotten mad at her, because she'd told him he shouldn't have turned the cat into a cat-rug, and although he had always obeyed her more than anyone else, which was hardly at all, this time he'd snapped at her. With his mind. And that had been the end of Amy Fremont's bright eyes, and the end of Amy Fremont as everyone had known her. And that was when word got around in Peaksville (population: 46) that even the members of Anthony's own family weren't safe. After that, everyone was twice as careful.

Someday Anthony might undo what he'd done to Aunt Amy. Anthony's Mom and Pop hoped he would. When he was older, and maybe sorry. If it was possible, that is. Because Aunt Amy had changed a lot, and besides, now Anthony wouldn't obey anyone.

"Land alive, William," Aunt Amy said, "you don't have to mumble like that. Anthony wouldn't hurt you. My goodness, Anthony likes you!" She raised her voice and called to Anthony, who had tired of the rat and was making it eat itself. "Don't you, dear? Don't you like Mr. Soames?"

Anthony looked across the lawn at the grocery man —a bright, wet, purple gaze. He didn't say anything. Bill Soames tried to smile at him. After a second Anthony returned his attention to the rat. It had already devoured its tail, or at least chewed it off— for Anthony had made it bite faster than it could swallow, and little pink and red furry pieces lay around it on the green grass. Now the rat was having trouble reaching its hindquarters.

Mumbling silently, thinking of nothing in particular as hard as he could, Bill Soames went stiff-legged down the walk, mounted his bicycle and pedalled off.

"We'll see you tonight, William," Aunt Amy called after him.

As Bill Soames pumped the pedals, he was wishing deep down that he could pump twice as fast, to get away from Anthony all the faster, and away from Aunt Amy, who sometimes just forgot how *careful* you had to be. And he shouldn't have thought that. Because Anthony caught it. He caught the desire to get away from the Fremont house as if it was something *bad*, and his purple gaze blinked, and he snapped a small, sulky thought after Bill Soames—just a small one, because he was in a good mood today, and besides, he liked Bill Soames, or at least didn't dislike him, at least today. Bill Soames wanted to go away—so, petulantly, Anthony helped him.

Pedalling with superhuman speed—or rather, appearing to, because in reality the bicycle was pedalling *him*—Bill Soames vanished down the road in a cloud of dust, his thin, terrified wail drifting back across the summerlike heat.

Anthony looked at the rat. It had devoured half its belly, and had died from pain. He thought it into a grave out deep in the cornfield—his father had once said, smiling, that he might as well do that with the things he killed—and went around the house, casting his odd shadow in the hot, brassy light from above.

In the kitchen, Aunt Amy was unpacking the groceries. She put the Mason-jarred goods on the shelves, and the meat and milk in the icebox, and the beet sugar and coarse flour in big cans under the sink. She put the cardboard box in the corner, by the door, for Mr. Soames to pick up next time he came. It was stained and battered and torn and worn fuzzy, but it was one of the few left in Peaksville. In faded red letters it said *Campbell's Soup.* The last cans of soup, or of anything else, had been eaten long ago, except for a small communal hoard which the villagers dipped into for special occasions—but the box lingered on, like a coffin, and when it and the other boxes were gone, the men would have to make some out of wood.

Aunt Amy went out in back, where Anthony's Mom —Aunt Amy's sister—sat in the shade of the house, shelling peas. The peas, every time Mom ran a finger along a pod, went *lollop-lollop-lollop* into the pan on her lap.

"William brought the groceries," Aunt Amy said. She sat down wearily in the straightbacked chair beside Mom, and began fanning herself again. She wasn't really old; but ever since Anthony had snapped at her with his mind, something had seemed to be wrong with her body as well as her mind, and she was tired all the time.

"Oh, good," said Mom. *Lollop* went the fat peas into the pan.

Everybody in Peaksville always said "Oh, fine," or "Good," or "Say, that's swell!" when almost anything happened or was mentioned—even unhappy things like accidents or even deaths. They'd always say "Good," because if they didn't try to cover up how they really felt, Anthony might overhear with his mind, and then nobody knew what might happen. Like the time Mrs. Kent's husband, Sam, had come walking back from the graveyard, because Anthony liked Mrs. Kent and had heard her mourning.

Lollop.

"Tonight's television night," said Aunt Amy. "I'm

glad. I look forward to it so much every week. I wonder what we'll see tonight?"

"Did Bill bring the meat?" asked Mom.

"Yes." Aunt Amy fanned herself, looking up at the featureless brassy glare of the sky. "Goodness, it's so hot! I wish Anthony would make it just a little cooler—"

"_Amy!_"

"Oh!" Mom's sharp tone had penetrated, where Bill Soames' agonized expression had failed. Aunt Amy put one thin hand to her mouth in exaggerated alarm. "Oh . . . I'm sorry, dear." Her pale blue eyes shuttled around, right and left, to see if Anthony was in sight. Not that it would make any difference if he was or wasn't—he didn't have to be near you to know what you were thinking. Usually, though, unless he had his attention on somebody, he would be occupied with thoughts of his own.

But some things attracted his attention—you could never be sure just what.

"This weather's just _fine_," Mom said.

Lollop.

"Oh, yes," Aunt Amy said. "It's a wonderful day. I wouldn't want it changed for the world!"

Lollop.

Lollop.

"What time is it?" Mom asked.

Aunt Amy was sitting where she could see through the kitchen window to the alarm clock on the shelf above the stove. "Four-thirty," she said.

Lollop.

"I want tonight to be something special," Mom said. "Did Bill bring a good lean roast?"

"Good and lean, dear. They butchered just today, you know, and sent us over the best piece."

"Dan Hollis will be *so* surprised when he finds out that tonight's television party is a birthday party for him too!"

"Oh, *I* think he will! Are you sure nobody's told him?"

"Everybody swore they wouldn't."

"That'll be real nice," Aunt Amy nodded, looking off across the cornfield. "A birthday party."

"Well—" Mom put the pan of peas down beside her, stood up and brushed her apron. "I'd better get the roast on. Then we can set the table." She picked up the peas.

Anthony came around the corner of the house. He didn't look at them, but continued on down through the carefully kept garden—*all* the gardens in Peaksville were carefully kept, very carefully kept—and went past the rusting, useless hulk that had been the Fremont family car, and went smoothly over the fence and out into the cornfield.

"Isn't this a lovely day!" said Mom, a little loudly, as they went towards the back door.

Aunt Amy fanned herself. "A beautiful day, dear. Just *fine!*"

Out in the cornfield, Anthony walked between the tall, rustling rows of green stalks. He liked to smell the corn. The alive corn overhead, and the old dead corn underfoot. Rich Ohio earth, thick with weeds and brown, dry-rotting ears of corn, pressed between his bare toes with every step—he had made it rain last night so everything would smell and feel nice today.

He walked clear to the edge of the cornfield, and over to where a grove of shadowy green trees covered

cool, moist, dark ground, and lots of leafy undergrowth, and jumbled moss-covered rocks, and a small
spring that made a clear, clean pool. Here Anthony
liked to rest and watch the birds and insects and small
animals that rustled and scampered and chirped about.
He liked to lie on the cool ground and look up through
the moving greenness overhead, and watch the insects
flit in the hazy soft sunbeams that stood like slanting,
glowing bars between ground and treetops. Somehow,
he liked the thoughts of the little creatures in this
place better than the thoughts outside; and while the
thoughts he picked up here weren't very strong or very
clear, he could get enough out of them to know what
the little creatures liked and wanted, and he spent a
lot of time making the grove more like what they
wanted it to be. The spring hadn't always been here;
but one time he had found thirst in one small furry
mind, and had brought subterranean water to the
surface in a clear cold flow, and had watched blinking
as the creature drank, feeling its pleasure. Later he had
made the pool, when he found a small urge to swim.

He had made rocks and trees and bushes and caves,
and sunlight here and shadows there, because he had
felt in all the tiny minds around him the desire—or
the instinctive want—for this kind of resting place,
and that kind of mating place, and this kind of place
to play, and that kind of home.

And somehow the creatures from all the fields and
pastures around the grove had seemed to know that
this was a good place, for there were always more of
them coming in—every time Anthony came out here
there were more creatures than the last time, and more
desires and needs to be tended to. Every time there
would be some kind of creature he had never seen

before, and he would find its mind, and see what it wanted, and then give it to it.

He liked to help them. He liked to feel their simple gratification.

Today, he rested beneath a thick elm, and lifted his purple gaze to a red and black bird that had just come to the grove. It twittered on a branch over his head, and hopped back and forth, and thought its tiny thoughts, and Anthony made a big, soft nest for it, and pretty soon it hopped in.

A long, brown, sleek-furred animal was drinking at the pool. Anthony found its mind next. The animal was thinking about a smaller creature that was scurrying along the ground on the other side of the pool, grubbing for insects. The little creature didn't know that it was in danger. The long, brown animal finished drinking and tensed its legs to leap, and Anthony thought it into a grave in the cornfield.

He didn't like those kinds of thoughts. They reminded him of the thoughts outside the grove. A long time ago some of the people outside had thought that way about *him,* and one night they'd hidden and waited for him to come back from the grove—and he'd just thought them all into the cornfield. Since then, the rest of the people hadn't thought that way—at least, very clearly. Now their thoughts were all mixed up and confusing whenever they thought about him or near him, so he didn't pay much attention.

He liked to help them too, sometimes—but it wasn't simple, or very gratifying either. They never thought happy thoughts when he did—just the jumble. So he spent more time out here.

He watched all the birds and insects and furry creatures for a while, and played with a bird, making it soar and dip and streak madly around tree trunks until, accidentally, when another bird caught his attention for a moment, he ran it into a rock. Petulantly, he thought the rock into a grave in the cornfield; but he couldn't do anything more with the bird. Not because it was dead, though it was; but because it had a broken wing. So he went back to the house. He didn't feel like walking back through the cornfield, so he just *went* to the house, right down into the basement.

It was nice down here. Nice and dark and damp and sort of fragrant, because once Mom had been making preserves in a rack along the far wall, and then she'd stopped coming down ever since Anthony had started spending time here, and the preserves had spoiled and leaked down and spread over the dirt floor, and Anthony liked the smell.

He caught another rat, making it smell cheese, and after he played with it, he thought it into a grave right beside the long animal he'd killed in the grove. Aunt Amy hated rats, and so he killed a lot of them, because he liked Aunt Amy most of all and sometimes did things that Aunt Amy wanted. Her mind was more like the little furry minds out in the grove. She hadn't thought anything bad at all about him for a long time.

After the rat, he played with a big black spider in the corner under the stairs, making it run back and forth until its web shook and shimmered in the light from the cellar window like a reflection in silvery water. Then he drove fruit flies into the web until the spider was frantic trying to wind them all up. The spider liked flies, and its thoughts were stronger than theirs, so he did it. There was something bad in the way it liked flies, but it wasn't clear—and besides, Aunt Amy hated flies too.

He heard footsteps overhead—Mom moving around in the kitchen. He blinked his purple gaze, and almost decided to make her hold still—but instead he *went* up to the attic, and, after looking out the circular window at the front end of the long V-roofed room for a while at the front lawn and the dusty road and Henderson's tip-waving wheatfield beyond, he curled into an unlikely shape and went partly to sleep.

Soon people would be coming for television, he heard Mom think.

He went more to sleep. He liked television night. Aunt Amy had always liked television a lot, so one time he had thought some for her, and a few other people had been there at the time, and Aunt Amy had felt disappointed when they wanted to leave. He'd done something to them for that—and now everybody came to television.

He liked all the attention he got when they did.

Anthony's father came home around six-thirty, looking tired and dirty and bloody. He'd been over in Dunn's pasture with the other men, helping pick out the cow to be slaughtered this month and doing the job, and then butchering the meat and salting it away in Soames's icehouse. Not a job he cared for, but every man had his turn. Yesterday, he had helped scythe down old McIntyre's wheat. Tomorrow, they would start threshing. By hand. Everything in Peaksville had to be done by hand.

He kissed his wife on the cheek and sat down at the kitchen table. He smiled and said, "Where's Anthony?"

"Around someplace," Mom said.

Aunt Amy was over at the wood-burning stove, stirring the big pot of peas. Mom went back to the oven and opened it and basted the roast.

"Well, it's been a *good* day," Dad said. By rote. Then he looked at the mixing bowl and breadboard on the table. He sniffed at the dough. "M'm," he said. "I could eat a loaf all by myself, I'm so hungry."

"No one told Dan Hollis about its being a birthday party, did they?" his wife asked.

"Nope. We kept as quiet as mummies."

"We've fixed up such a lovely surprise!"

"Um? What?"

"Well . . . you know how much Dan likes music. Well, last week Thelma Dunn found a *record* in her attic!"

"No!"

"Yes! And we had Ethel sort of ask—you know, without really *asking*—if he had that one. And he said no. Isn't that a wonderful surprise?"

"Well, now, it sure is. A record, imagine! That's a real nice thing to find! What record is it?"

"Perry Como, singing 'You Are My Sunshine'."

"Well, I'll be darned. I always liked that tune." Some raw carrots were lying on the table. Dad picked up a small one, scrubbed it on his chest, and took a bite. "How did Thelma happen to find it?"

"Oh, you know—just looking around for new things."

"M'm." Dad chewed the carrot. "Say, who has that picture we found a while back? I kind of liked it— that old clipper sailing along—"

"The Smiths. Next week the Sipichs get it, and they give the Smiths old McIntyre's music-box, and we give the Sipichs—" and she went down the tentative order of things that would exchange hands among the women at church this Sunday.

He nodded. "Looks like we can't have the picture for a while, I guess. Look, honey, you might try to get that detective book back from the Reillys. I was so busy the week we had it, I never got to finish all the stories—"

"I'll try," his wife said doubtfully. "But I hear the van Husens have a stereoscope they found in the cellar." Her voice was just a little accusing. "They had it two whole months before they told anybody about it—"

"Say," Dad said, looking interested. "That'd be nice, too. Lots of pictures?"

"I suppose so. I'll see on Sunday. I'd like to have it —but we still owe the van Husens for their canary. I don't know why that bird had to pick *our* house to die . . . it must have been sick when we got it. Now there's just no satisfying Betty van Husen—she even hinted she'd like our *piano* for a while!"

"Well, honey, you try for the stereoscope—or just anything you think we'll like." At last he swallowed the carrot. It had been a little young and tough. Anthony's whims about the weather made it so that people never knew what crops would come up, or what shape they'd be in if they did. All they could do was plant a lot; and always enough of something came up any one season to live on. Just once there had been a grain surplus; tons of it had been hauled to the edge of Peaksville and dumped off into the nothingness. Otherwise, nobody could have breathed, when it started to spoil.

"You know," Dad went on. "It's nice to have the new things around. It's nice to think that there's probably still a lot of stuff nobody's found yet, in cellars and attics and barns and down behind things. They help, somehow. As much as anything can help—"

"Sh-h!" Mom glanced nervously around.

"Oh," Dad said, smiling hastily. "It's all right! The new things are *good!* It's *nice* to be able to have something around you've never seen before, and know that something you've given somebody else is making them happy . . . that's a real *good* thing."

"A good thing," his wife echoed.

"Pretty soon," Aunt Amy said, from the stove, "there won't be any more new things. We'll have found everything there is to find. Goodness, that'll be too bad—"

"*Amy!*"

"Well—" her pale eyes were shallow and fixed, a sign of her recurrent vagueness. "It will be kind of a shame—no new things—"

"Don't *talk* like that," Mom said, trembling. "Amy, be *quiet!*"

"It's *good,*" said Dad, in the loud, familiar, wanting-to-be-overheard tone of voice. "Such talk is *good.* It's okay, honey—don't you see? It's good for Amy to talk any way she wants. It's good for her to feel bad. Everything's good. Everything *has* to be good. . . ."

Anthony's mother was pale. And so was Aunt Amy —the peril of the moment had suddenly penetrated the clouds surrounding her mind. Sometimes it was difficult to handle words so that they might not prove disastrous. You just never *knew.* There were so many things it was wise not to say, or even think—but remonstration for saying or thinking them might be just as bad, if Anthony heard and decided to do anything about it. You could just never tell what Anthony was liable to do.

Everything had to be good. Had to be fine just as it was, even if it wasn't. Always. Because any change might be worse. So terribly much worse.

"Oh, my goodness, yes, of course it's good," Mom said. "You talk any way you want to, Amy, and it's just fine. Of course, you want to remember that some ways are *better* than others. . . ."

Aunt Amy stirred the peas, fright in her pale eyes.

"Oh, yes," she said. "But I don't feel like talking right now. It . . . it's *good* that I don't feel like talking."

Dad said tiredly, smiling, "I'm going out and wash up."

They started arriving around eight o'clock. By that time, Mom and Aunt Amy had the big table in the dining-room set, and two more tables off to the side. The candles were burning, and the chairs situated, and Dad had a big fire going in the fireplace.

The first to arrive were the Sipichs, John and Mary. John wore his best suit, and was well-scrubbed and pink-faced after his day in McIntyre's pasture. The suit was neatly pressed, but getting threadbare at elbows and cuffs. Old McIntyre was working on a loom, designing it out of schoolbooks, but so far it was slow going. McIntyre was a capable man with wood and tools, but a loom was a big order when you couldn't get metal parts. McIntyre had been one of the ones who, at first, had wanted to try to get Anthony to make things the villagers needed, like clothes and canned goods and medical supplies and gasoline. Since then, he felt that what had happened to the whole Terrance family and Joe Kinney was his fault, and he worked hard trying to make it up to the rest of them. And since then, no one had tried to get Anthony to do anything.

Mary Sipich was a small, cheerful woman in a simple dress. She immediately set about helping Mom and Aunt Amy put the finishing touches on the dinner.

The next arrivals were the Smiths and the Dunns, who lived right next to each other down the road, only a few yards from the nothingness. They drove up in the Smiths' wagon, drawn by their old horse.

Then the Reillys showed up, from across the darkened wheatfield, and the evening really began. Pat Reilly sat down at the big upright in the front room, and began to play from the popular sheet music on the rack. He played softly, as expressively as he could —and nobody sang. Anthony liked piano playing a whole lot, but not singing; often he would come up from the basement, or down from the attic, or just _come,_ and sit on top of the piano, nodding his head as Pat played "Lover" or "Boulevard of Broken Dreams" or "Night and Day." He seemed to prefer ballads, sweet-sounding songs—but the one time somebody had started to sing, Anthony had looked over from the top of the piano and done something that made everybody afraid of singing from then on. Later, they'd decided that the piano was what Anthony had heard first, before anybody had ever tried to sing, and now anything else added to it didn't sound right and distracted him from his pleasure.

So, every television night, Pat would play the piano, and that was the beginning of the evening. Wherever Anthony was, the music would make him happy, and put him in a good mood, and he would know that they were gathering for television and waiting for him.

By eight-thirty everybody had shown up, except for

the seventeen children and Mrs. Soames who was off watching them in the schoolhouse at the far end of town. The children of Peaksville were never, never allowed near the Fremont house—not since little Fred Smith had tried to play with Anthony on a dare. The younger children weren't even told about Anthony. The others had mostly forgotten about him, or were told that he was a nice, nice goblin but they must never go near him.

Dan and Ethel Hollis came late, and Dan walked in not suspecting a thing. Pat Reilly had played the piano until his hands ached—he'd worked pretty hard with them today—and now he got up, and everybody gathered around to wish Dan Hollis a happy birthday.

"Well, I'll be darned," Dan grinned. "This is swell. I wasn't expecting this at all . . . gosh, this is *swell!*"

They gave him his presents—mostly things they had made by hand, though some were things that people had possessed as their own and now gave him as his. John Sipich gave him a watch charm, hand-carved out of a piece of hickory wood. Dan's watch had broken down a year or so ago, and there was nobody in the village who knew how to fix it, but he still carried it around because it had been his grandfather's and was a fine old heavy thing of gold and silver. He attached the charm to the chain, while everybody laughed and said John had done a nice job of carving. Then Mary Sipich gave him a knitted necktie, which he put on, removing the one he'd worn.

The Reillys gave him a little box they had made, to keep things in. They didn't say what things, but Dan said he'd keep his personal jewellery in it. The Reillys had made it out of a cigar box, carefully peeled off its paper and lined it on the inside with velvet. The outside had been polished, and carefully if not expertly carved by Pat—but his carving got complimented too. Dan Hollis received many other gifts—a pipe, a pair of shoelaces, a tie pin, a knit pair of socks, some fudge, a pair of garters made from old suspenders.

He unwrapped each gift with vast pleasure, and wore as many of them as he could right there, even the garters. He lit up the pipe, and said he'd never had a better smoke; which wasn't quite true, because the pipe wasn't broken in yet. Pete Manners had had it lying around ever since he'd received it as a gift four years ago from an out-of-town relative who hadn't known he'd stopped smoking.

Dan put the tobacco into the bowl very carefully. Tobacco was precious. It was only pure luck that Pat Reilly had decided to try to grow some in his backyard just before what had happened to Peaksville had happened. It didn't grow very well, and then they had to cure it and shred it and all, and it was just precious stuff. Everybody in town used wooden holders old McIntyre had made, to save on butts.

Last of all, Thelma Dunn gave Dan Hollis the record she had found.

Dan's eyes misted even before he opened the package. He knew it was a record.

"Gosh," he said softly. "What one is it? I'm almost afraid to look . . ."

"You haven't got it, darling," Ethel Hollis smiled. "Don't you remember, I asked about 'You Are My Sunshine'?"

"Oh, gosh," Dan said again. Carefully he removed the wrapping and stood there fondling the record, running his big hands over the worn grooves with their tiny, dulling crosswise scratches. He looked around the room, eyes shining, and they all smiled back, knowing how delighted he was.

"Happy birthday, darling!" Ethel said, throwing her arms around him and kissing him.

He clutched the record in both hands, holding it off to one side as she pressed against him. "Hey," he laughed, pulling back his head. "Be careful . . . I'm holding a priceless object!" He looked around again, over his wife's arms, which were still around his neck. His eyes were hungry. "Look . . . do you think we could play it? Lord, what I'd give to hear some new music . . . just the first part, the orchestra part, before Como sings?"

Faces sobered. After a minute, John Sipich said, "I don't think we'd better, Dan. After all, we don't know just where the singer comes in—it'd be taking too much of a chance. Better wait till you get home."

Dan Hollis reluctantly put the record on the buffet with all his other presents. "It's *good*," he said automatically, but disappointedly, "that I can't play it here."

"Oh, yes," said Sipich. "It's good." To compensate for Dan's disappointed tone, he repeated, "It's *good*."

They ate dinner, the candles lighting their smiling faces, and ate it all right down to the last delicious drop of gravy. They complimented Mom and Aunt Amy on the roast beef, and the peas and carrots, and the tender corn on the cob. The corn hadn't come from the Fremont's cornfield, naturally—everybody knew what was out there; and the field was going to weeds.

Then they polished off the dessert—homemade ice cream and cookies. And then they sat back, in the flickering light of the candles, and chatted, waiting for television.

There never was a lot of mumbling on television night—everybody came and had a good dinner at the Fremonts', and that was nice, and afterwards there was television, and nobody really thought much about that—it just had to be put up with. So it was a pleasant enough get-together, aside from your having to watch what you said just as carefully as you always did every place. If a dangerous thought came into your mind, you just started mumbling, even right in the middle of a sentence. When you did that, the others just ignored you until you felt happier again and stopped.

Anthony liked television night. He had done only two or three awful things on television night in the whole past year.

Mom had put a bottle of brandy on the table, and they each had a tiny glass of it. Liquor was even more precious than tobacco. The villagers could make wine, but the grapes weren't right, and certainly the techniques weren't, and it wasn't very good wine. There were only a few bottles of real liquor left in the village —four rye, three Scotch, three brandy, nine real wine and half a bottle of Drambuie belonging to old McIntyre (only for marriages)—and when those were gone, that was it.

Afterward, everybody wished that the brandy hadn't been brought out. Because Dan Hollis drank more of it than he should have, and mixed it with a lot of the homemade wine. Nobody thought anything about it at first, because he didn't show it much outside, and it was his birthday party and a happy party, and Anthony liked these get-togethers and shouldn't see any reason to do anything even if he was listening.

But Dan Hollis got high, and did a fool thing. If they'd seen it coming, they'd have taken him outside and walked him around.

The first thing they knew, Dan stopped laughing right in the middle of the story about how Thelma Dunn had found the Perry Como record and dropped it and it hadn't broken because she'd moved faster than she ever had before in her life and caught it. He was fondling the record again, and looking longingly at the Fremonts' gramophone over in the corner, and suddenly he stopped laughing and his face got slack, and then it got ugly, and he said, "Oh, *Christ!*"

Immediately the room was still. So still they could hear the whirring movement of the grandfather's clock out in the hall. Pat Reilly had been playing the piano, softly. He stopped, his hands poised over the yellowed keys.

The candles on the dining-room table flickered in a cool breeze that blew through the lace curtains over the bay window.

"Keep playing, Pat," Anthony's father said softly.

Pat started again. He played "Night and Day," but his eyes were sidewise on Dan Hollis, and he missed notes.

Dan stood in the middle of the room, holding the record. In his other hand he held a glass of brandy so hard his hand shook.

They were all looking at him.

"*Christ,*" he said again, and he made it sound like a dirty word.

Reverend Younger, who had been talking with Mom

and Aunt Amy by the dining-room door, said "Christ"
too—but he was using it in a prayer. His hands were
clasped, and his eyes were closed.

John Sipich moved forward. "Now, Dan . . . it's
good for you to talk that way. But you don't want to
talk too much, you know."

Dan shook off the hand Sipich put on his arm.

"Can't even play my record," he said loudly. He
looked down at the record, and then around at their
faces. "Oh, my *God* . . ."

He threw the glassful of brandy against the wall. It
splattered and ran down the wallpaper in streaks.

Some of the women gasped.

"Dan," Sipich said in a whisper. "Dan, cut it out—"

Pat Reilly was playing "Night and Day" louder, to
cover up the sounds of the talk. It wouldn't do any
good, though, if Anthony was listening.

Dan Hollis went over to the piano and stood by
Pat's shoulder, swaying a little.

"Pat," he said. "Don't play *that*. Play *this*." And
he began to sing. Softly, hoarsely, miserably: "Happy
birthday to me . . . Happy birthday to me. . . ."

"*Dan!*" Ethel Hollis screamed. She tried to run
across the room to him. Mary Sipich grabbed her arm
and held her back. "Dan," Ethel screamed again.
"Stop—"

"My God, be quiet!" hissed Mary Sipich, and
pushed her towards one of the men, who put his hand
over her mouth and held her still.

"—Happy birthday, dear Danny," Dan sang.
"Happy birthday to me!" He stopped and looked
down at Pat Reilly. "Play it, Pat. Play it, so I can sing
right . . . you know I can't carry a tune unless somebody plays it!"

Pat Reilly put his hands on the keys and began "Lover"—in a slow waltz tempo, the way Anthony liked it. Pat's face was white. His hands fumbled.

Dan Hollis stared over at the dining-room door. At Anthony's mother, and at Anthony's father who had gone to join her.

"*You* had him," he said. Tears gleamed on his cheeks as the candlelight caught them. "*You* had to go and *have* him. . . ."

He closed his eyes, and the tears squeezed out. He sang loudly, "You are my sunshine . . . my only sunshine . . . you make me happy . . . when I am blue. . . ."

Anthony *came* into the room.

Pat stopped playing. He froze. Everybody froze. The breeze rippled the curtains. Ethel Hollis couldn't even try to scream—she had fainted.

"Please don't take my sunshine . . . away . . ." Dan's voice faltered into silence. His eyes widened. He put both hands out in front of him, the empty glass in one, the record in the other. He hiccupped, and said, "*No—*"

"Bad man," Anthony said, and thought Dan Hollis into something like nothing anyone would have believed possible, and then he thought the thing into a grave deep, deep in the cornfield.

The glass and record thumped on the rug. Neither broke.

Anthony's purple gaze went around the room.

Some of the people began mumbling. They all tried to smile. The sound of mumbling filled the room like a far-off approval. Out of the murmuring came one or two clear voices:

"Oh, it's a very *good* thing," said John Sipich.

"A good thing," said Anthony's father, smiling. He'd had more practice in smiling than most of them. "A wonderful thing."

"It's swell . . . just swell," said Pat Reilly, tears leaking from eyes and nose, and he began to play the piano again, softly, his trembling hands feeling for "Night and Day."

Anthony climbed up on top of the piano, and Pat played for two hours.

Afterwards, they watched television. They all went into the front room, and lit just a few candles, and pulled up chairs around the set. It was a small-screen set, and they couldn't all sit close enough to it to see, but that didn't matter. They didn't even turn the set on. It wouldn't have worked anyway, there being no electricity in Peaksville.

They just sat silently, and watched the twisting, writhing shapes on the screen, and listened to the sounds that came out of the speaker, and none of them had any idea of what it was all about. They never did. It was always the same.

"It's real nice," Aunt Amy said once, her pale eyes on the meaningless flickers and shadows. "But I liked it a little better when there were cities outside and we could get real—"

"Why, Amy!" said Mom. "It's good for you to say such a thing. Very good. But how can you mean it? Why, this television is *much* better than anything we ever used to get!"

"Yes," chimed in John Sipich. "It's fine. It's the best show we've ever seen!"

He sat on the couch, with two other men, holding

Ethel Hollis flat against the cushions, holding her arms and legs and putting their hands over her mouth, so she couldn't start screaming again.

"It's really *good!*" he said again.

Mom looked out of the front window, across the darkened road, across Henderson's darkened wheat field to the vast, endless, grey nothingness in which the little village of Peaksville floated like a soul—the huge nothingness that was most evident at night, when Anthony's brassy day had gone.

It did no good to wonder where they were . . . no good at all. Peaksville was just someplace. Someplace away from the world. It was wherever it had been since that day three years ago when Anthony had crept from her womb and old Doc Bates—God rest him—had screamed and dropped him and tried to kill him, and Anthony had whined and done the thing. Had taken the village someplace. Or had destroyed the world and left only the village, nobody knew which.

It did no good to wonder about it. Nothing at all did any good—except to live as they must live. Must always, always live, if Anthony would let them.

These thoughts were dangerous, she thought.

She began to mumble. The others started mumbling too. They had all been thinking, evidently.

The men on the couch whispered and whispered to Ethel Hollis, and when they took their hands away, she mumbled too.

While Anthony sat on top of the set and made television, they sat around and mumbled and watched the meaningless, flickering shapes far into the night.

Next day it snowed, and killed off half the crops—but it was a *good* day.

FRANK STOCKTON

The Transferred Ghost

*"Yes, I am his ghost," my companion replied, "and
yet I have no right to be."*

The country residence of Mr. John Hinckman was
a delightful place to me, for many reasons. It was
the abode of a genial, though somewhat impulsive,
hospitality. It had broad, smooth-shaven lawns and
towering oaks and elms; there were bosky shades at
several points, and not far from the house there was a
little rill spanned by a rustic bridge with the bark on;
there were fruits and flowers, pleasant people, chess,
billiards, rides, walks, and fishing. These were great
attractions; but none of them, nor all of them together,
would have been sufficient to hold me to the place very
long. I had been invited for the trout season, but
should, probably, have finished my visit early in the
summer had it not been that upon fair days, when the

grass was dry, and the sun was not too hot, and there was but little wind, there strolled beneath the lofty elms, or passed lightly through the bosky shades, the form of my Madeline.

This lady was not, in very truth, my Madeline. She had never given herself to me, nor had I, in any way, acquired possession of her. But as I considered her possession the only sufficient reason for the continuance of my existence, I called her, in my reveries, mine. It may have been that I would not have been obliged to confine the use of this possessive pronoun to my reveries had I confessed the state of my feelings to the lady.

But this was an unusually difficult thing to do. Not only did I dread, as almost all lovers dread, taking the step which would in an instant put an end to that delightful season which may be termed the ante-interrogatory period of love, and which might at the same time terminate all intercourse or connection with the object of my passion; but I was, also, dreadfully afraid of John Hinckman. This gentleman was a good friend of mine, but it would have required a bolder man than I was at that time to ask him for the gift of his niece, who was the head of his household, and, according to his own frequent statement, the main prop of his declining years. Had Madeline acquiesced in my general views on the subject, I might have felt encouraged to open the matter to Mr. Hinckman; but, as I said before, I had never asked her whether or not she would be mine. I thought of these things at all hours of the day and night, particularly the latter.

I was lying awake one night, in the great bed in my spacious chamber, when, by the dim light of the new moon, which partially filled the room, I saw John

Hinckman standing by a large chair near the door. I was very much surprised at this for two reasons. In the first place, my host had never before come into my room; and, in the second place, he had gone from home that morning, and had not expected to return for several days. It was for this reason that I had been able that evening to sit much later than usual with Madeline on the moonlit porch. The figure was certainly that of John Hinckman in his ordinary dress, but there was a vagueness and indistinctness about it which presently assured me that it was a ghost. Had the good old man been murdered? and had his spirit come to tell me of the deed, and to confide to me the protection of his dear —? My heart fluttered at what I was about to think, but at this instant the figure spoke.

"Do you know," he said, with a countenance that indicated anxiety, "if Mr. Hinckman will return to-night?"

I thought it well to maintain a calm exterior, and I answered,—

"We do not expect him."

"I am glad of that," said he, sinking into the chair by which he stood. "During the two years and a half that I have inhabited this house, that man has never before been away for a single night. You can't imagine the relief it gives me."

And as he spoke he stretched out his legs, and leaned back in the chair. His form became less vague, and the colors of his garments more distinct and evident, while an expression of gratified relief succeeded to the anxiety of his countenance.

"Two years and a half!" I exclaimed. "I don't understand you."

"It is fully that length of time," said the ghost,

"since I first came here. Mine is not an ordinary case. But before I say any thing more about it, let me ask you again if you are sure Mr. Hinckman will not return to-night."

"I am as sure of it as I can be of any thing," I answered. "He left to-day for Bristol, two hundred miles away."

"Then I will go on," said the ghost, "for I am glad to have the opportunity of talking to some one who will listen to me; but if John Hinckman should come in and catch me here, I should be frightened out of my wits."

"This is all very strange," I said, greatly puzzled by what I had heard. "Are you the ghost of Mr. Hinckman?"

This was a bold question, but my mind was so full of other emotions that there seemed to be no room for that of fear.

"Yes, I am his ghost," my companion replied, "and yet I have no right to be. And this is what makes me so uneasy, and so much afraid of him. It is a strange story, and, I truly believe, without precedent. Two years and a half ago, John Hinckman was dangerously ill in this very room. At one time he was so far gone that he was really believed to be dead. It was in consequence of too precipitate a report in regard to this matter that I was, at that time, appointed to be his ghost. Imagine my surprise and horror, sir, when, after I had accepted the position and assumed its responsibilities, that old man revived, became convalescent, and eventually regained his usual health. My situation was now one of extreme delicacy and embarrassment. I had no power to return to my original unembodiment, and I had no right to be the ghost of a man who was not dead. I was advised by my friends to quietly maintain my position, and was assured that, as John Hinckman was an elderly man, it could not be long before I could rightfully assume the position for which I had been selected. But I tell you, sir," he continued, with animation, "the old fellow seems as vigorous as ever, and I have no idea how much longer this annoying state of things will continue. I spend my time trying to get out of that old man's way. I must not leave this house, and he seems to follow me everywhere. I tell you, sir, he haunts me."

"That is truly a queer state of things," I remarked. "But why are you afraid of him? He couldn't hurt you."

"Of course he couldn't," said the ghost. "But his very presence is a shock and terror to me. Imagine, sir, how you would feel if my case were yours."

I could not imagine such a thing at all. I simply shuddered.

"And if one must be a wrongful ghost at all," the apparition continued, "it would be much pleasanter to be the ghost of some man other than John Hinckman. There is in him an irascibility of temper, accompanied by a facility of invective, which is seldom met with. And what would happen if he were to see me, and find out, as I am sure he would, how long and why I had inhabited his house, I can scarcely conceive. I have seen him in his bursts of passion; and, although he did not hurt the people he stormed at any more than he would hurt me, they seemed to shrink before him."

All this I knew to be very true. Had it not been for this peculiarity of Mr. Hinckman, I might have been more willing to talk to him about his niece.

"I feel sorry for you," I said, for I really began to

have a sympathetic feeling toward this unfortunate apparition. "Your case is indeed a hard one. It reminds me of those persons who have had doubles, and I suppose a man would often be very angry indeed when he found that there was another being who was personating himself."

"Oh! the cases are not similar at all," said the ghost. "A double or doppelganger lives on the earth with a man; and, being exactly like him, he makes all sorts of trouble, of course. It is very different with me. I am not here to live with Mr. Hinckman. I am here to take his place. Now, it would make John Hinckman very angry if he knew that. Don't you know it would?"

I assented promptly.

"Now that he is away I can be easy for a little while," continued the ghost; "and I am so glad to have an opportunity of talking to you. I have frequently come into your room, and watched you while you slept, but did not dare to speak to you for fear that if you talked with me Mr. Hinckman would hear you, and come into the room to know why you were talking to yourself."

"But would he not hear you?" I asked.

"Oh, no!" said the other: "there are times when any one may see me, but no one hears me except the person to whom I address myself."

"But why did you wish to speak to me?" I asked.

"Because," replied the ghost, "I like occasionally to talk to people, and especially to some one like yourself, whose mind is so troubled and perturbed that you are not likely to be frightened by a visit from one of us. But I particularly wanted to ask you to do me a favor. There is every probability, so far as I can see, that John Hinckman will live a long time, and my situation is becoming insupportable. My great object at present is to get myself transferred, and I think that you may, perhaps, be of use to me."

"Transferred!" I exclaimed. "What do you mean by that?"

"What I mean," said the other, "is this: Now that I have started on my career I have got to be the ghost of somebody, and I want to be the ghost of a man who is really dead."

"I should think that would be easy enough," I said. "Opportunities must continually occur."

"Not at all! not at all!" said my companion quickly. "You have no idea what a rush and pressure there is for situations of this kind. Whenever a vacancy occurs, if I may express myself in that way, there are crowds of applications for the ghostship."

"I had no idea that such a state of things existed," I said, becoming quite interested in the matter. "There ought to be some regular system, or order of precedence, by which you could all take your turns like customers in a barber's shop."

"Oh dear, that would never do at all!" said the other. "Some of us would have to wait forever. There is always a great rush whenever a good ghostship offers itself—while, as you know, there are some positions that no one would care for. And it was in consequence of my being in too great a hurry on an occasion of the kind that I got myself into my present disagreeable predicament, and I have thought that it might be possible that you would help me out of it. You might know of a case where an opportunity for a ghostship was not generally expected, but which might present itself at any moment. If you would give me a short notice, I know I could arrange for a transfer."

"What do you mean?" I exclaimed. "Do you want me to commit suicide? Or to undertake a murder for your benefit?"

"Oh, no, no, no!" said the other, with a vapory smile. "I mean nothing of that kind. To be sure, there are lovers who are watched with considerable interest, such persons having been known, in moments of depression, to offer very desirable ghostships; but I did not think of any thing of that kind in connection with you. You were the only person I cared to speak to, and I hoped that you might give me some information that would be of use; and, in return, I shall be very glad to help you in your love affair."

"You seem to know that I have such an affair," I said.

"Oh, yes!" replied the other, with a little yawn. "I could not be here so much as I have been without knowing all about that."

There was something horrible in the idea of Madeline and myself having been watched by a ghost, even, perhaps, when we wandered together in the most delightful and bosky places. But, then, this was quite an exceptional ghost, and I could not have the objections to him which would ordinarily arise in regard to beings of his class.

"I must go now," said the ghost, rising: "but I will see you somewhere to-morrow night. And remember— you help me, and I'll help you."

I had doubts the next morning as to the propriety of telling Madeline any thing about this interview, and soon convinced myself that I must keep silent on the subject. If she knew there was a ghost about the house, she would probably leave the place instantly. I did not

mention the matter, and so regulated my demeanor
that I am quite sure Madeline never suspected what
had taken place. For some time I had wished that Mr.
Hinckman would absent himself, for a day at least,
from the premises. In such case I thought I might more
easily nerve myself up to the point of speaking to
Madeline on the subject of our future collateral existence; and, now that the opportunity for such speech
had really occurred, I did not feel ready to avail myself of it. What would become of me if she refused
me?

I had an idea, however, that the lady thought that, if
I were going to speak at all, this was the time. She must
have known that certain sentiments were afloat within
me, and she was not unreasonable in her wish to see the
matter settled one way or the other. But I did not feel
like taking a bold step in the dark. If she wished me to
ask her to give herself to me, she ought to offer me
some reason to suppose that she would make the gift.
If I saw no probability of such generosity, I would prefer that things should remain as they were.

That evening I was sitting with Madeline in the
moonlit porch. It was nearly ten o'clock, and ever since
supper-time I had been working myself up to the point
of making an avowal of my sentiments. I had not
positively determined to do this, but wished gradually
to reach the proper point, when, if the prospect looked
bright, I might speak. My companion appeared to
understand the situation—at least, I imagined that the
nearer I came to a proposal the more she seemed to
expect it. It was certainly a very critical and important
epoch in my life. If I spoke, I should make myself happy

or miserable forever; and if I did not speak I had every reason to believe that the lady would not give me another chance to do so.

Sitting thus with Madeline, talking a little, and thinking very hard over these momentous matters, I looked up and saw the ghost, not a dozen feet away from us. He was sitting on the railing of the porch, one leg thrown up before him, the other dangling down as he leaned against a post. He was behind Madeline, but almost in front of me, as I sat facing the lady. It was fortunate that Madeline was looking out over the landscape, for I must have appeared very much startled. The ghost had told me that he would see me some time this night, but I did not think he would make his appearance when I was in the company of Madeline. If she should see the spirit of her uncle, I could not answer for the consequences. I made no exclamation, but the ghost evidently saw that I was troubled.

"Don't be afraid," he said—"I shall not let her see me; and she cannot hear me speak unless I address myself to her, which I do not intend to do."

I suppose I looked grateful.

"So you need not trouble yourself about that," the ghost continued; "but it seems to me that you are not getting along very well with your affair. If I were you, I should speak out without waiting any longer. You will never have a better chance. You are not likely to be interrupted; and, so far as I can judge, the lady seems disposed to listen to you favorably; that is, if she ever intends to do so. There is no knowing when John Hinckman will go away again; certainly not this summer. If I were in your place, I should never dare to make love to Hinckman's niece if he were anywhere about the place. If he should catch any one offering himself to Miss Madeline, he would then be a terrible man to encounter."

I agreed perfectly to all this.

"I cannot bear to think of him!" I ejaculated aloud.

"Think of whom?" asked Madeline, turning quickly toward me.

Here was an awkward situation. The long speech of the ghost, to which Madeline paid no attention, but which I heard with perfect distinctness, had made me forget myself.

It was necessary to explain quickly. Of course, it would not do to admit that it was of her dear uncle that I was speaking; and so I mentioned hastily the first name I thought of.

"Mr. Vilars," I said.

This statement was entirely correct; for I never could bear to think of Mr. Vilars, who was a gentleman who had, at various times, paid much attention to Madeline.

"It is wrong for you to speak in that way of Mr. Vilars," she said. "He is a remarkably well educated and sensible young man, and has very pleasant manners. He expects to be elected to the legislature this fall, and I should not be surprised if he made his mark. He will do well in a legislative body, for whenever Mr. Vilars has any thing to say he knows just how and when to say it."

This was spoken very quietly, and without any show of resentment, which was all very natural, for if Madeline thought at all favorably of me she could not feel displeased that I should have disagreeable emotions in regard to a possible rival. The concluding words contained a hint which I was not slow to understand. I felt very sure that if Mr. Vilars were in my present position he would speak quickly enough.

"I know it is wrong to have such ideas about a person," I said, "but I cannot help it."

The lady did not chide me, and after this she seemed even in a softer mood. As for me, I felt considerably annoyed, for I had not wished to admit that any thought of Mr. Vilars had ever occupied my mind.

"You should not speak aloud that way," said the ghost, "or you may get yourself into trouble. I want to see every thing go well with you, because then you may be disposed to help me, especially if I should chance to be of any assistance to you, which I hope I shall be."

I longed to tell him that there was no way in which he could help me so much as by taking his instant departure. To make love to a young lady with a ghost sitting on the railing near by, and that ghost the apparition of a much-dreaded uncle, the very idea of whom in such a position and at such a time made me tremble, was a difficult, if not an impossible, thing to do; but I forbore to speak, although I may have looked my mind.

"I suppose," continued the ghost, "that you have not heard any thing that might be of advantage to me. Of course, I am very anxious to hear; but if you have any thing to tell me, I can wait until you are alone. I will come to you to-night in your room, or I will stay here until the lady goes away."

"You need not wait here," I said; "I have nothing at all to say to you."

Madeline sprang to her feet, her face flushed and her eyes ablaze.

"Wait here!" she cried. "What do you suppose I am waiting for? Nothing to say to me indeed!—I

232

should think so! What should you have to say to me?"

"Madeline," I exclaimed, stepping toward her, "let me explain."

But she had gone.

Here was the end of the world for me! I turned fiercely to the ghost.

"Wretched existence!" I cried. "You have ruined every thing. You have blackened my whole life. Had it not been for you"—

But here my voice faltered. I could say no more.

"You wrong me," said the ghost. "I have not injured you. I have tried only to encourage and assist you, and it is your own folly that has done this mischief. But do not despair. Such mistakes as these can be explained. Keep up a brave heart. Good-by."

And he vanished from the railing like a bursting soap-bubble.

I went gloomily to bed, but I saw no apparitions that night except those of despair and misery which my wretched thoughts called up. The words I had uttered had sounded to Madeline like the basest insult. Of course, there was only one interpretation she could put upon them.

As to explaining my ejaculations, that was impossible. I thought the matter over and over again as I lay awake that night, and I determined that I would never tell Madeline the facts of the case. It would be better for me to suffer all my life than for her to know that the ghost of her uncle haunted the house. Mr. Hinckman was away, and if she knew of his ghost she could not be made to believe that he was not dead. She might not survive the shock! No, my heart could bleed, but I would never tell her.

The next day was fine, neither too cool nor too

warm; the breezes were gentle, and nature smiled. But there were no walks or rides with Madeline. She seemed to be much engaged during the day, and I saw but little of her. When we met at meals she was polite, but very quiet and reserved. She had evidently determined on a course of conduct, and had resolved to assume that, although I had been very rude to her, she did not understand the import of my words. It would be quite proper, of course, for her not to know what I meant by my expressions of the night before.

I was downcast and wretched, and said but little, and the only bright streak across the black horizon of my woe was the fact that she did not appear to be happy, although she affected an air of unconcern. The moonlit porch was deserted that evening, but wandering about the house I found Madeline in the library alone. She was reading, but I went in and sat down near her. I felt that, although I could not do so fully, I must in a measure explain my conduct of the night before. She listened quietly to a somewhat labored apology I made for the words I had used.

"I have not the slightest idea what you meant," she said, "but you were very rude."

I earnestly disclaimed any intention of rudeness, and assured her, with a warmth of speech that must have made some impression upon her, that rudeness to her would be an action impossible to me. I said a great deal upon the subject, and implored her to believe that if it were not for a certain obstacle I could speak to her so plainly that she would understand every thing.

She was silent for a time, and then she said, rather more kindly, I thought, than she had spoken before:

234

"Is that obstacle in any way connected with my uncle?"

"Yes," I answered, after a little hesitation, "it is, in a measure, connected with him."

She made no answer to this, and sat looking at her book, but not reading. From the expression of her face, I thought she was somewhat softened toward me. She knew her uncle as well as I did, and she may have been thinking that, if he were the obstacle that prevented my speaking (and there were many ways in which he might be that obstacle), my position would be such a hard one that it would excuse some wildness of speech and eccentricity of manner. I saw, too, that the warmth of my partial explanations had had some effect on her, and I began to believe that it might be a good thing for me to speak my mind without delay. No matter how she should receive my proposition, my relations with her could not be worse than they had been the previous night and day, and there was something in her face which encouraged me to hope that she might forget my foolish exclamations of the evening before I began to tell her my tale of love.

I drew my chair a little nearer to her, and as I did so the ghost burst into the room from the door-way behind her. I say burst, although no door flew open and he made no noise. He was wildly excited, and waved his arms above his head. The moment I saw him, my heart fell within me. With the entrance of that impertinent apparition, every hope fled from me. I could not speak while he was in the room.

I must have turned pale; and I gazed steadfastly at the ghost, almost without seeing Madeline, who sat between us.

"Do you know," he cried, "that John Hinckman is coming up the hill? He will be here in fifteen minutes; and if you are doing any thing in the way of love-making, you had better hurry it up. But this is not what I came to tell you. I have glorious news! At last I am transferred! Not forty minutes ago a Russian nobleman was murdered by the Nihilists. Nobody ever thought of him in connection with an immediate ghost-ship. My friends instantly applied for the situation for me, and obtained my transfer. I am off before that horrid Hinckman comes up the hill. The moment I reach my new position, I shall put off this hated semblance. Good-by. You can't imagine how glad I am to be, at last, the real ghost of somebody."

"Oh!" I cried, rising to my feet, and stretching out my arms in utter wretchedness, "I would to Heaven you were mine!"

"I *am* yours," said Madeline, raising to me her tearful eyes.

Biographical Notes

Biographical Notes

COMPILED BY SHERRY KNOX

JOHN BELL CLAYTON (*1906–1955*), *American*
The White Circle, *page 3*

Clayton was born on a farm in the mountainous region of Virginia, west of the Blue Ridge. He spent several years at the University of Virginia, leaving to become a reporter on a small daily newspaper. Although he worked for a while as a publicist, and held a job with the Federal Communications Commission during World War II, he spent most of his working years as a newspaperman. He was the author of two novels, *Six Angels at My Back,* and *Wait Son, October Is Near,* and a collection of short sories, *The Strangers Were There.*

MARY E. WILKINS (*1852–1930*), *American*
The Wind in the Rose-Bush, *page 14*

With Sarah Orne Jewett, Mary Wilkins was considered one of the last great New England genre writers. She came from old Massachusetts stock, and after a rather haphazard education became secretary to Oliver Wendell Holmes, Sr., through whom she met many of the prominent writers of the day. In 1891 she gained recognition in her own right with the publication of "A New England Nun." By the time of her death she had written 238 short stories, 12 novels, 1 play and 2 volumes of verse. She wrote about the daily frustrations of village life, which she described with simplicity, frankness, and a dry sense of humor.

Biographical Notes

WILKIE COLLINS (*1824–1889*), *English*
Blow Up with the Brig!, *page 37*

The meeting of Wilkie Collins and Charles Dickens in 1851 was of real significance to the history of literature as well as to their own careers. Dickens was a master of characterization; Collins could devise a superlative plot. Many critics agree that their best works reflect the strengths of the other. Collins became one of Dickens' most intimate friends and a regular contributor to his publications. In 1868 Collins published *The Moonstone,* a work which T. S. Eliot has called "the first and greatest of English detective novels," and which gained Collins his reputation as "father of the English detective story." Other novels include *The Woman in White* (1860), *The New Magdalen* (1873), and *The Haunted Hotel* (1879).

D'ARCY NILAND (*1920–1967*), *Australian*
The Web, *page 55*

Before becoming a full-time writer, Niland worked as a magazine editor, special correspondent, and roving journalist. He was born and educated in New South Wales, where he spent most of his life. His most successful novel was *The Shiralee* (1955), which was published in twelve languages and made into a motion picture. Besides his novels and short stories, Niland wrote newspaper articles and a number of television scripts. At the time of his death he was at work on a biography of Les Darcy, an Australian prizefighter.

JACK LONDON (*1876–1916*), *American*
To Build a Fire, *page 64*

A novelist and short-story writer, London was born in San Francisco, the illegitimate child of an Irish astrologer and a Wisconsin farm woman. At ten he was borrowing books of adventure and travel from the Oakland Public Library and working odd jobs on paper routes, ice wagons, and in the jute mills; at fifteen he went on the road as a tramp, riding the blinds across the Sierra Nevadas; at twenty he trekked to the Klondike, with thousands of others, to mine gold. He returned to California without having mined an ounce, but with experience later chronicled in *The Call of the Wild,* a novel which sold 1.5 million copies in 1903. Later novels included *The Sea Wolf* (1904), *Martin Eden* (1909; an autobiographical novel), and *John Barleycorn* (1913).

ROBERT LOUIS STEVENSON (*1850–1894*), *Scottish*
The Body-Snatcher, page 87

Stevenson was born in Edinburgh of strict Calvinistic stock. His father, Thomas, came of a celebrated line of lighthouse builders, and his plan was that his son should follow in this tradition as an engineer. Robert, however, wanted to be a man of letters. In 1875 he took up residence at Barbizon, in the Forest of Fontainebleau, where he lived in an artists' colony. During the next fifteen years he produced his best essays, and novels, and firmly established his career. *Treasure Island* was published in the periodical *Young Folks; Dr. Jekyll and Mr. Hyde* (1886) sold 40,000 copies in six months; and *Kidnapped* (1886) also had a great success. In 1887 Stevenson made a second trip to America, then traveled to the South Seas where he settled in Samoa and where, four years later, he died.

VIN PACKER *American*
Only the Guilty Run, page 113

Vin Packer is the pseudonym of Marijane Meaker, author of more than twenty suspense novels. She also writes children's books under the name of M. E. Kerr. Born in Auburn, New York, she attended school in Virginia and graduated from the University of Missouri in 1950. Her most recent works are *Don't Rely on Gemini,* published by Delacorte Press in 1969; and *Shockproof Sydney Skate,* which Little, Brown published in 1972.

Biographical Notes

JULIAN HAWTHORNE (*1846–1934*), *American*
My Friend Paton, *page 127*

Hawthrone was born in Boston, the only son of novelist Nathaniel Hawthorne and his wife, Sophia (Peabody) Hawthorne. Julian Hawthorne's novels, many of them sensational and fantastic, represented a transition between the Gothic romanticism of early American novels and the scientific naturalism of later periods. In the 1880s he developed a new variant of the detective story, using the real-life experiences of the famous New York Inspector Byrnes in "The Great Bank Robbery," "An American Penman," and other stories. Besides his novels, Hawthorne was a prolific writer of popular histories and syndicated articles.

A. M. BURRAGE (*b. 1889*), *English*
Playmates, *page 151*

While still in school, Burrage began to write and sell his stories; became a professional writer at the early age of seventeen. He served in France during the First World War and later contributed stories, articles and poems to over 150 publications, among them *Strand, Sketch,* and *Tatler.* His works, some published under pseudonyms (Ex Private X is one of them), include *The Smokes of Spring* (1926); *Some Ghost Stories* (1927); and *Someone in the Room* (1931).

HUGH PENTECOST (*b. 1903*), *American*
My Dear Uncle Sherlock, *page 184*

Pentecost is the pen name of Judson Philips, who acted in silent films opposite such stars as Elaine Hammerstein and Olive Thomas, and later began writing for the pulp magazines that flourished during the 1920s and '30s. In 1939 he won the Dodd, Mead mystery contest with a novel called *Cancelled in Red;* and thus Hugh Pentecost was born. In his early career he wrote mainly fiction based on factual backgrounds; later, he developed several series characters. He has published over fifty suspense novels; stories for magazines; and scripts for radio, television, and film.

JEROME BIXBY (*b. 1923*), *American*
It's a Good Life, page 196

Bixby is a science-fiction writer who has been editor of *Planet Stories* and *Galaxy*. He co-authored, with Otto Klement, the original script of the motion picture *Fantastic Voyage,* which was later novelized by Issac Asimov. "It's a Good Life" has been translated and adapted for television. Bixby has written such other tales as "The Bad Life," "The Monsters," and "Halfway to Hell."

FRANK STOCKTON (*1834–1902*), *American*
The Transferred Ghost, page 221

Frank Stockton's career as a humorist was launched in 1879 with the publication of the novel *Rudder Grange.* This story, about an amusing maidservant, Pomona, was an immediate success and was followed by *The Rudder Grangers Abroad* and *Pomona's Travels.* Stockton was also a gifted short-story writer and caused a sensation with "The Lady and the Tiger," which first appeared in the November 1882 issue of *Century.* Over the years, he was associated with many periodicals, first with *Riverside Magazine for Young People,* then with *Hearth and Home* and *Scribner's Magazine.* Beside his short stories, novels, and articles, he wrote a book on European travel and, in collaboration with his wife, a household handbook.

JOAN KAHN has been hailed as the wizard of mystery editors and is well-known for the Harper Novels of Suspense and for her anthologies of suspense stories, which include *Some Things Strange and Sinister, Some Things Dark and Dangerous,* and *The Edge of the Chair.* She is the author of several books for children and two adult novels.

A native New Yorker, Joan Kahn was graduated from the Horace Mann School and later attended Barnard College, the Yale Art School, and the Art Students' League. She is an editor with a leading publishing house and lives in New York City.